KENNY'S BACK

by

I0665122

Victor J. Banis

The Borgo Press
An Imprint of Wildside Press

MMVII

SECOND EDITION

CONTENTS

ABOUT THE AUTHOR

*Lecturer, former writing instructor and early rabble-rouser for gay rights and freedom of the press, **VICTOR J. BANIS** is the critically acclaimed author ("...a master storyteller"—*Publishers Weekly*) of more than 140 published novels and nonfiction works, and his verse and short pieces have appeared in numerous journals (*Blithe House Quarterly, *Fall 2006*) and anthologies (*Charmed Lives, *Lethe Press, 2006*).*

CHAPTER ONE

Kenny was back. I think the whole town knew it and waited for the event as breathlessly and fearfully as we in the pink house did. The October stillness that had fallen upon us seemed to grow more intense as the day approached, until all of Hanover hovered in suspended animation.

He planned it that way, of course—the drama of waiting, expecting, not knowing—so that his appearance, when it came, was as much a shock as though we had not known he was coming. It was his same sense of drama, undoubtedly, that dictated the manner in which, almost at the end of the day, he did finally appear. He could as well have called from the station or, more simply, let us know when he would arrive. And for our part, it would not have been hard to determine the hour. Not so many trains or busses stop at Hanover, after all. But, just as in the past, we followed his cue, and waited at the house.

He was there at last, strolling up the lane with an almost brazen nonchalance, as though five years and a storm of scandal and heartbreak had not passed since the last such stroll. It was a shock to see him wearing the faded Levis and the battered suede jacket, so shabby and unflattering, which he had worn constantly before, even when, as now, it was too warm for such garb.

It was staged, yes, and calculated to erase the time that had passed; and in that it was effective. Later I would see him at closer range and talk to him, and there would be time to see that things had, after all, changed. But for now, standing at the second story window, seeing his approach only in an accidental way as I happened to glance from the window, I fell victim to his ruse. And I admit it: I was as enchanted by him as I—and everyone—had always been.

If I had let myself, I would have burst from the room, run down the stairs and out of the house; I would have met him in the lane, and we'd have walked together to the house as we used to do, and talk of what he'd done in town, or the omens that the weather harbored. We might even have quarreled—we had done enough of that, too, in the past, although I was not alone in that distinction. Whom *hadn't* Kenny quarreled with? With some, God forgive it, far more bitterly than with me.

I nearly did just that, run to him. I was to the door before I caught myself. It was my face that stopped me, or rather its reflection in the mirror: flushed red, my eyes wide and brilliant with excitement, my lips wet where I had unconsciously run my tongue over them, a sure sign of my nervousness.

I stopped short and stared hard at that excited face in the mirror, and knew it would never do to let him see me like this.

"Mar," I said to myself, but aloud, "You stupid Swede, don't be a fool."

That settled me down a bit, long enough at least to take stock. I'd come in just before from the far fields, where the last of the hay was being baled. I was sweaty and dirty, and my damnably fair skin was burnt from the sun. I was shirtless beneath the dirty bib overalls, so big for me that they made me look more like a clown than a farmhand.

"Well, he won't be expecting a Mississippi gambler," I told myself, laughing at my own silliness. I didn't add that, for all I knew, he wouldn't be expecting me at all, or care whether I was there or not. I took time enough to put on a shirt under the bib, and I spit on my hand and slicked down the cowlick that he had teased me about in the past.

"Kenny's here," I told the reflection. Not, "Kenny's back," but "Kenny's here," and the reflection laughed at me silently.

6

Strange, that after that awful strained day of waiting, Kenny almost made it to the house without being noticed. I must have been the first to see him, at least the first of those who had watched all day. The alarm wasn't sounded until I was halfway down the stairs from my room, and I heard Ingrid's excited yell, "Kenny's here." The door slammed after her and I could picture her racing down the lane toward him, probably looking more like the girl of seventeen he had left behind than the young lady of twenty-two she had become.

She had reached him long before I came out of the front door and paused on the porch, looking across the big front yard toward them. He caught her up in his arms to kiss her, and swung her around lightly and easily.

"He's still strong," I thought with a smile, remembering how, even as a kid, he'd been stronger than he looked. He seemed taller than I remembered him. Somehow I'd always pictured him as never reaching any higher than my shoulder, and even at the distance I could see he was taller than that now. He was still thin, in that lithe way of his, not skinny or frail, but wiry and tight-fleshed, like a wildcat that hasn't an ounce of flesh more than what he needs. He was a little paler, too, although still dark, with that raven-colored hair flopping over his forehead, and those eyes, so dark they looked like midnight, peering out below that.

They started across the yard together, Kenny and Ingrid, talking at the same time to one another, laughing as they had laughed together when they were kids. He still had that indolent grace to his movements, more pronounced now, I thought—but I reminded myself that he was probably nervous too. He'd have to be, no matter how hard he pretended. He'd always pretended, and when he was most scared, he'd act the surest and swagger the most.

There were a few of the hands about, but none of them knew him. The ones he had known had come and gone, and were replaced now by new faces. Except for Pete, who had come around the corner of the house. He stopped there, just waiting, but I knew that beneath the disinterested air he assumed, Pete was as excited as anyone. Maybe he wasn't sure just yet, nearly blind as he was, but his face showed nothing, and he made no move to intercept the route that Ingrid and Kenny were taking across the yard.

"Here's Pete," Ingrid said, close enough by now that I could hear her voice. For a moment, I thought Kenny would ignore her comment. He had looked up just then to the porch. My mother had come out of the house too, standing beside me drying her hands on a dishtowel. He looked at her, still laughing at something Ingrid had said in a smaller voice. Then his eyes moved on to me and for a fraction of a second I thought the smile faded, to be replaced by an expression I couldn't identify.

It was gone as quickly as it had come, if it had existed at all, ended by Ingrid's voice. Kenny turned and saw Pete, and they veered in that direction, hurrying toward the old man. Kenny let go of Ingrid and clasped Pete's hand, shaking it with warm enthusiasm—and I knew that things had changed after all in those five years.

Not a handshake, I thought, sharing the surprise and the hurt I knew Pete must feel behind that impassive face. *Never a handshake*. Even after he had grown up and become a young man, Kenny had never had but one greeting for the old fellow he had idolized so, who'd entertained him with his countless yarns. I tried to think what Pete must be feeling, after all those times of being embraced by those husky young arms, squeezed until, as he put it, his ribs creaked. And now, after five years to himself, with no one to listen avidly to his yarns, he had gotten a handshake from the boy he had loved as a son.

But he's not a boy, I reminded myself. The five years between eighteen and twenty-three are long ones, and a boy becomes a man who shakes hands with people he used to embrace, and kisses girls he used to tease.

I almost turned and went back in the house. Suddenly I didn't want to see how he greeted farmhands he used to Indian-wrestle with, and go bare-ass swimming with. But I stayed, because he had looked back in our direction and started toward us, grinning so that every one of those white teeth was shining in the sunlight. Ingrid was frowning, though. She knew he had changed too, I thought.

"Olsen." He greeted my mother first, almost shyly, and then bounded up the wooden steps to grab her roughly in his arms.

"Welcome home," she said with a break in her voice. "Welcome home, Kenny."

I'd probably have been jealous before, in the vague way I had always been when I knew that he was her favorite. We were her children, Ingrid and I, and he the boss's son, but he had always been her pet, and she his.

"Ingemar."

It didn't register at first. I was staring right at him, waiting for him to greet me, and I saw him look at me and hold out his hand—but I'd never heard that name from him before, and it sounded foreign and strange, like he was talking to someone else—so much so that I almost turned to see who was behind me.

"Mar," he corrected himself, grinning from ear to ear.

I took his hand then, and returned his shake, but I felt a little of what Pete must have felt. "Welcome back," I said, smiling and trying to show no feelings except pleasure at seeing him. I must not have succeeded altogether, because I saw Ingrid's face over his shoulder and for a brief instant she looked pale and—frightened almost. Kenny didn't notice anything, though. In the past, Kenny had noticed everything. He'd always known just what everyone was feeling or thinking.

"It's good to be back," he said to the three of us at once. He put an arm around each of the women, squeezing again as though to assure himself that it was real. He sniffed, wrinkling up his nose in an exaggerated manner as he turned his head back and forth, like a hound on the scent.

"I'm starving," he declared. "And you've been baking, Olsen."

"Apple pie," she answered, beaming with motherly pride.

"What's the occasion?" he asked, his eyes twinkling with mischief.

"Oh, you," she said, poking him and freeing herself from his embrace. "I've a mind to let the hogs have it, they always were more grateful than some."

He's afraid, I thought again, seeing him glance in the direction of the screen door. *He's got the worst yet before him, and he wishes it didn't have to be done.*

Olsen—I'd picked up that name from Kenny, and she had always been Olsen to me too, never "Mother"—Olsen had seen the glance too, and they grew sober together.

"She didn't come out," he said bluntly, looking straight into Olsen's eyes.

She flushed slightly under the frank gaze. "Your mother's not been well," she said. "There've been times of late when I thought..." She left unsaid what she had thought, but he understood.

"She knows I'm here?"

"She knew you were coming. Lands, I'd think the whole county would have heard Ingrid's yelping." She twisted the dishtowel nervously in her hands, but she did not look away from him, or back down before his stare.

"Will she see me?" It must have been a hard question to ask, especially when you had to ask it about your own mother.

"I think she will. I think she wants to. But she's been sick, awful sick. If she doesn't see you just now, you mustn't think...well, she might not be strong enough just yet."

"I understand," he said quietly. She seemed relieved by the answer.

"I'll tell her you're here," Ingrid offered, moving toward the door.

"No." Olsen stopped her. "No, I'll do it. You take Kenny into the kitchen. I'll bet he could use some coffee. And Mar, too."

"I'm starving, and she offers me coffee," he protested.

"We eat at six." No amount of excitement was likely to cause a change in the schedule by which Olsen ran her kitchen. Not even Kenny's return would change that.

"Still plug up the holes with cotton, I see," Kenny commented as he held the screen door open for her and poked one of the white tufts that filled the holes where the screen had rusted out.

10

"Keeps the flies out," she said, talking over her shoulder as she went in. "Not the oats bugs, though. They was worse than ever this year, like to ate us alive."

"It's your cooking draws them,' he said, letting Ingrid go in before him. He gave me a wink as he followed her, a wink that was just as devilish as it had ever been, five years or no.

For a moment I was left on the porch alone, staring at the screen door and its cotton tufts. Kenny was back. Whether he would stay or not depended upon what happened inside, upon the meeting that was still to come. I didn't even want to guess what it would be like. I hoped it would be easy and more pleasant than their last one. I hoped that for her sake, that frail old creature waiting inside, knowing, surely, that he was here, and perhaps as frightened as he was. I hoped it for his sake as well—and for my own, too, although I tried not to think about that.

It seemed as if I had a lot that I was trying not to think of just now. I was trying not to remember what it was like to hold a naked young man in my arms. I was holding back the memories, a threatening flood of them, of those times with him, of the feel and taste of another man's cock, of his ass with the springy cheeks, and what it felt like to be in there, fucking him. Even the smell of him, clean but not spicy, an honest male smell of sweat and hot flesh and muscle—I was trying to forget that, too.

It was pretty silly for me to remember any of it. Especially those times Kenny; and I had shared, when the emotional and physical merged to fill us both with an overwhelming passion. It hurt now to remember, yet the call of the past was strong and sweet and I tested it, feeling my cock stir in response as my mind skittered over many scenes, then settled on one.

Kenny and I were stretched out naked by the swimming hole. The day was hot and we had splashed and played for an hour. Kenny's body sparkled with droplets of water. I stretched on my side and looked at him as he lay on his back, eyes closed, his hard, lean body bare. I could see the sun drying his skin, tiny bubbles bursting and disappearing as a larger expanse of dryness started at his chest and moved across his flat belly.

I loved looking at him. My eyes traveled downward to his cock and it was as if my own erotic thoughts had become his. He grew hard. His cock rose as I watched it. Our thoughts had been transferred. We were that close, that deeply bound to each other in mind and body.

Kenny stretched his arms over his head, and turned and faced me. He grinned. For some reason, I was suddenly embarrassed.

"It's good, isn't it, Mar?" Kenny asked

"What's good?" I asked, already knowing he was going to say something about us, and how we were together.

"It's good we're so damn close," he said.

"Yes, it is," I answered. I looked into his eyes, but I still carried a half-vision of his risen cock.

Neither of us said anything more. It wasn't necessary. In a moment, and in a manner that was quite spontaneous, Kenny hiked his body closer to me. We were both on our sides, facing each other, close, but not in contact until Kenny took a deep breath. Then I felt the tip of his cock touch mine. It was as if we were joined by a single organ, as if his belonged to me and mine belonged to him and we both belonged to this single element of our lust and love. It was scary, and it was exciting. And beautiful. I didn't want the feeling ever to leave me. But I knew it would. Kenny was that way. Any excitement, regardless of its beauty, had to be increased. In a second, Kenny moved to increase it.

"I'm going to jerk you off, Mar," he said softly. We had done that before, together, but never to one another.

I leaned back a little. Kenny bowed to my thighs, paused a moment, then gripped my cock lightly at the base and began to stroke it.

I moaned. I couldn't help it. I wanted to feel what Kenny was feeling too, and I wanted him to feel what I was feeling. I shifted a bit, and reached for his cock, so that we could do it together.

Kenny stopped me, though. He was jerking it hard now but, without losing a stroke, he pressured against me, signaling me to lie still. I did. This would be one of those

12

times when Kenny only gave, without receiving in like quality. I did not protest. He was always the one who ran this show. I remained as still as possible, giving myself up to the thrill he was creating.

He made me come very fast. I couldn't hold back. The ache started in my balls, then the tension released, and Kenny continued it until I was drained dry, and limp, a mere fraction of myself still held lightly between his fingers.

It had been different for us that time. Much different, but good, like all our times together were good. Nearly all, anyway. Some weren't so good.

I stirred from my memory. Yes, I thought, it was silly for me to remember. All those time, and all those memories staying with me—and Kenny hadn't even remembered my name, not the name he had always called me. All the times that I had wished Kenny were with me, that we could fuck again.

Well, he was back now and, in a way, I guess I had my wish: I really felt like I had been screwed.

KENNY'S BACK, BY VICTOR J. BANIS

CHAPTER TWO

Strange, we had waited in tense excitement, not only that day, but I think through the whole time he was gone, for Kenny to come back. Olsen and Ingrid had cleaned that house until every inch of it glistened, and Olsen had practically worked herself into a lather cooking and baking every single dish she could think of that Kenny had ever liked. It was like a son returning from the wars, a prodigal son, and that night should have been a time of celebration and high spirits. But all we had done was gather the wood and the kindling, and we had heaped it plenty high enough, all right, but the match that was needed to set it blazing was missing.

I was the first to see Olsen come into the kitchen, and I knew from her pale face and hot red eyes that the meeting we were all waiting for wasn't going to take place—not this night, at least. Kenny's back was to her and when she put her hand lightly on his shoulder, he jumped high enough that he all but scraped the ceiling. I had never seen or imagined Kenny that tense.

"Tomorrow," Olsen answered the question in his dark eyes. "She'll see you tomorrow. She's as weak as a kitten tonight."

I looked away when she said it. I didn't want to see the reaction in his face. But at least she hadn't sent him away, and she hadn't outright refused to see him. Olsen would never have lied about that, not even though she loved

15

Kenny as much as she did. So now we'd have to wait some more, for another day, at least.

All of us showed the strain of that waiting as the evening passed. I thought about all the things I could do to make it easier, if not for me, then at least for Kenny. I almost suggested showing him the barn, and some of the work we had done around the place since he had been gone. I thought of taking him into town for a beer or something. We had done that sometimes, even though back then Kenny hadn't been dry behind the ears. I thought of a dozen things we used to do on nights like this, when Kenny wasn't up to some mischief or wanted someone to share his mischief with him.

There was a wall five years thick between us, though, and I sat quietly and waited for Kenny; to come over it, or open a gate in it; but if there was such a gate, Kenny didn't find it, or else he passed it by without notice. The closest we came to conversation was when he remarked to me, "It sure is hot for October, isn't it?" and I said, "Spring came late."

It was Ingrid who kept things moving along. I don't know whether she alone escaped the strain of the evening or whether maybe she felt it worst of all, but she talked almost without stopping for a breath. Olsen had always said that what Ingrid lacked in things to say she made up for in words to say it with, but at least she filled up some of the empty spaces of that night with her words, and I think we were all glad for that.

Kenny talked too, and kidded around with her, but his heart wasn't in it any more than it was in the spread that Olsen set before us. I had seen Kenny many a time put away a whole apple pie without making a dent in his appetite, but this time he picked at the one piece like it was made of sawdust. At nine o'clock, at least two hours earlier than I had ever known him to think of bed—at least, for sleeping—he yawned.

"It's been a long day," he said in a voice that came as close as he had ever let it come to apologizing.

"I'll show you your room," Ingrid said, jumping up from her chair.

He fixed a peculiar look on her, one that I couldn't make out. "I haven't forgotten it," he said simply. He stood up then and started from the room alone.

"See you all in the morning," he said, and he was gone.

I smiled to myself at that. How had the little devil known that the old room was still his? It was the nicest bedroom in the house and it might well have been taken over by one of us in the years that he had been gone, instead of being kept like a shrine for him. But he had known—and as usual, he had been right.

"He hasn't changed a bit," Ingrid said, looking after him with a wistful expression.

Olsen snorted in the funny way she had and busied herself clearing the rest of the table. "As though you had sense enough to notice," she commented, but in such a way that said she didn't mean it.

"Funny, I'd forgotten how handsome he was," Ingrid said. She chewed at the knuckle of one hand, a habit we both shared, and stared thoughtfully at the door through which he had gone. She remembered me finally and turned her blue eyes on me almost accusingly.

"Mar, aren't you happy to see him back?" she asked. "You've been as quiet as a parson in a brothel."

"Ingrid." Olsen banged a bowl into the sink disapprovingly.

"Well, he has," she insisted.

"It's his home, isn't it?" I replied, standing up and avoiding Ingrid's eyes. "This I where he ought to be. Some day he'll own all this, if…" I shrugged and didn't finish it. We all knew that whether he would ever own it or not depended upon that meeting with his mother. It was no secret that for more than a year now Mrs. Baker had intended changing her will, when she was strong enough to deal with the lawyers. If she went ahead with those plans, it would be the church, and not Kenny, who would own the place someday.

"And if he does, what'll happen to us? What'll happen to you, Mar?" Ingrid asked in a cooler voice. "You might not be running things then, Mar. At best you'd be just another hired hand."

That stopped me. Even Olsen, at the sink, turned around with a shocked expression. I suppose both of us still thought of Ingrid as young and sweet, forgetting that she could also be spiteful and mean.

The worst of it was, though, that she was right, even if I had never thought of that before. If Kenny stayed and patched things up with his mother, he would end up running the farm in place of me—and I would be just another hired hand, or maybe out of a job altogether.

"Is that why you were so cold toward him?" Ingrid asked cuttingly.

"Ingrid, may the good Lord forgive you for talking this way," Olsen said. She put a hand to her breast. It had always been hard for her to see that people had their selfish sides too, and it was a part of life she had never been able to cope with.

"No," I said, holding my own temper in check, but with some effort. "No, that's not why."

It wasn't until I had gone out, banging the back door behind me that I realized she had goaded me after all into admitting that I had been cold toward him. I even wondered if maybe she didn't know why. For all her giddiness and apparent helplessness, I knew full well Ingrid was as sharp as she was pretty. Even if she had been stone stupid, she'd have known about the other, about what had happened before Kenny left. I doubt if there was anyone in Hanover who didn't know about Dexter Holloman. If Ingrid still had a crush on Kenny, it wasn't because she didn't know about that—and there was no telling how much more she might know.

I thought about Dexter Holloman while I finished up my chores, and the thought of him made me shiver even though it was a warm night.

They, the others in the house, were waiting with anxious breath for the meeting that was going to take place tomorrow in the pink house. Right now, that was as far as any of us had thought about things.

18

But Dexter was there, hanging back in the dark part of all our thoughts. Sooner or later, planned or accidental, there was sure to be another meeting too—and in the long run, that one might be more important than the one between Kenny and his mother.

The house was quiet when I came back in. Ingrid must have gone to her room. Olsen was in the front room, mending. I looked in on her after I had locked up.

"Good night," I said from the doorway. "Don't strain your eyes with that."

She smiled faintly. "That's like saying don't squeeze the apples after they're already sauce." She looked up over her glasses. "She didn't mean what she said, Mar."

"I know she didn't," I lied.

She sighed and folded her hands thoughtfully over her sewing. "Lord willing, someday I'll see her married to some nice young man. That's what she needs. I always thought how nice it would be if she and Kenny…but there, now I'm talking like a wishful old woman."

"Don't stay up all night wishing." I grinned at her and left, climbing the stairs toward my room. It was always easy to forget that mothers were human, and there was Olsen being just a little small too, but in a nice way. And she was right: it would be nice for Ingrid if she and Kenny were to hit it off that way. Probably it would even be a good thing for Kenny, in the long run.

Well, when it came to that, I was being the smallest of all, wasn't I? It was Ingrid who was most responsible for Kenny's coming back, and who had done the most to try to patch things up between him and his mother. And Olsen wasn't the first mother to wish her daughter could marry the boss's son. But what excuse did I have for being jealous. Love wasn't prerogative.

I cleaned up and went to my own room, where I undressed in the dark and threw myself across the top of the bedclothes. I yawned a few times and tried to convince myself that I was dog-tired and would fall right asleep.

I didn't, of course. I lay in the dark and stared up at the ceiling where the shadows of the big pear tree's branches chased one another back and forth with each breeze.

He was here, in the house, in the next room. If I called out, he'd probably hear me. Maybe he would even come slipping along the hall as he sometimes used to, and we'd smoke a cigarette in the dark and talk seriously about things that only seem important at times like that. Maybe....

The hall floor creaked, but it was only Olsen, coming to bed. It wasn't until she had gone by and the door to her room had opened and closed that I realized how tight my breath was in my chest. I sat up, shaking a little, and lit a cigarette.

He won't be coming down that hall, I told myself firmly, almost enjoying the flash of pain it caused me. That was too many years and too many pains ago, and probably he had forgotten all about that, just as he had forgotten that I was Mar, and not Ingemar. He had outgrown what I had never quite learned to live with, and it was time now for me to stop kidding myself about it and pretending it had been different.

Kenny had changed. Well, what of it? That wasn't so unusual. I'd changed too, in a lot of ways. Olsen had grown absentminded and I was willing to bet her hair was a lot grayer than it looked to me. Ingrid had grown up and become what everyone said was a beautiful woman, even though I still saw her as a skinny little girl.

The only thing that hadn't changed was the past. All of those times that I kept remembering, they were just the way they had always been, even to our very first day in the pink house. I was seventeen then, and Kenny thirteen, but there was more than four years difference between us. He was everything that a boy should be: devilish and full of life and fun; and if losing his father the year before had saddened him, it had done it in ways that didn't show, except maybe in the way he attached himself to me right off. And although I wasn't much more than a kid myself, I probably seemed old enough to be a father to him, or at least an older brother. I had been the man of our family for some time already, and was as somber and grim a Swede as ever took over running a farm.

We were hired in a package. If the truth were known, Kenny's mother was probably being as much charitable as

20

she was practical. But even then Mrs. Baker wasn't a strong woman and she was a widow by that time, with this big farm and another smaller one to run, and no one to run it for her but a thirteen year old boy who worked hard enough when he wasn't hiking through the woods hunting critters or taking off for the swimming hole.

That was how we'd come here. Olsen was to run the house and I, with some understandable doubts on Mrs. Baker's part, would run the farm. Ingrid, well, she helped Olsen and tormented Kenny.

Even then the world revolved around Kenny. If things were hard, when bad weather threatened the crops, he'd work around the clock and weary the strongest hand. But let him hear that the catfish were good someplace, or let someone even hint at some bit of trouble he could be stirring up, and he was off and running. He would stand all of our hair on end, mine the straightest; and then, when we were the maddest and I was all for crating him up and dropping him in the creek after his catfish, in he'd saunter, as calm as the first day of May. I gave him credit: he never lied about things or ducked a question. He'd confess all in a way that said, "What are you upset about anyway? It was only an outhouse that I pushed over, and I didn't even know Mr. Craig was in it."

And of course, by the time he was done smiling at us and doing little favors for us, and fawning over us, we'd all be asking ourselves just what we had been so upset about. Except, while we were asking, he'd be off on some new mischief.

Or, if all else failed and he couldn't soothe our anger any other way, he'd put on a face a mile long and then we would hear, "Nobody cares about me," and the like, until we all felt sorry for having been mad and outdid one another showing him we did care. Olsen always said later that the only people who could afford to say such a thing were those who knew better. Kenny knew better, of course, but that didn't stop him from using it to get his way.

When did it change? When did Kenny stop being the little kid that kept me hopping, the little brother I'd never had, and become something else, something crazy and undreamed of? I remember all, every day, every minute we spent together, but I don't remember when it changed.

When the work was light, I'd many times go off with him, hiking and fishing. We found a cave, that was our place to escape from the world of work and responsibilities, and we spent hours there. Or we'd go swimming in the creek behind the pasture. I must have seen that bare ass of his a hundred times and never thought about anything more than walloping it when he made me mad, and he'd seen me raw as many times.

"Big Swede," he called me, and he'd never admit it, but the one thing that really got him was that I was bigger down below than he was. Never mind that I was older. He couldn't stand being second best in anything. I'd see him look down at himself and then at me, and frown.

"Look how big it's getting," he said over and over again. "I'll bet I'm bigger than you before the year's out." He never quite made it, even though he swore he had.

Somehow it changed. The horseplay wasn't just horseplay, and the wrestling tired us out more, so that we would lay for long times wrapped together and panting while we caught our breath—which got harder and harder to catch each time. I should have stopped it, I guess, being the older, but even though I was old in some ways, I was still a kid in my body.

I suppose a lot of it was just kid stuff. If you took any two young boys and put them on a farm, and sent them out wrestling and swimming naked together and let them become the closest of friends, the same thing would most likely happen. For Kenny, that's probably all it ever was. But I can't kid myself. Even from the first time anything happened, I knew I felt about him in a way that I had always expected I would feel about a woman someday. Afterward, after Kenny, I never felt that way about anyone else, man or woman. I was convinced that I never would—that I never could.

It started with the arguments about size. Not satisfied with seeing them soft, Kenny had to compare them hard, and even though I got a little shy about it, nothing would do but what he had to get his way. Two boys, all by themselves in a

22

cave in the woods, cocks hard—somehow they had to be gotten soft again.

I was scared after the first time, and a little guilty too, I guess, but not Kenny. That devil had found a new game that he liked best of all, and to be honest he had less and less trouble each time persuading me to play.

All we did at first was play with one another, and sometimes it really was more of a game than anything else. We still argued about size and such, and I doubt if Kenny was ever happier than the day he found out he could shoot further than I could.

It went on like that for a while and then it kind of died down. We both outgrew it a little, I suppose, although occasionally we still played around like that. I was twenty-one by this time, and even though I still enjoyed and looked forward to those games of ours, I kept telling myself I was past the age when guys should be playing around with other guys.

As for Kenny, he had discovered girls and, for a year or so, that made a big difference. Of course, he had no more trouble persuading his new partners to play games with him than he had with me, and I guess he tried out that sport to his satisfaction, and to the dismay of a number of girls, who sent him notes and called at the house and otherwise pursued him. Thankfully none of them came up with any more evidence of their foolishness than broken hearts.

I thought that our fooling around was over—and in a sense it was. There was one girl Kenny had worked on for longer than the others, six months in all. He was seventeen then, going on eighteen, and as handsome a Romeo I swear as ever prowled the Ohio farmland. During those six months, we'd had none of our playing around, and I had pretty well gotten used to the idea that it was sadly over.

Then one night he came home from a dance he had been to with this girl—I don't even remember her name now—and he came slipping down the hall to my room to wake me up and have a cigarette. Before, that would have been a sign that he wanted to play, but now I wasn't sure, so I made no move in that direction, and for a while he didn't either, but just lay there on the bed and smoked his cigarette and talked about a lot of little things.

"How'd you do with your girl?" I asked him finally, knowing by now that something was bothering him, but not knowing what.

"I made out," he answered with his usual frankness.

"Great," I said, without much enthusiasm.

"It's funny, Mar," he said, propping himself up on an elbow and looking at me in the moonlight that spilled through the window. "It's not the same with a girl as it is with you."

I laughed aloud at that. "I hope not," I said finally.

Kenny remained serious though, and even that was a little bit unusual. "No, I mean it," he insisted and then, after a pause, "Mar, do you want to? Now, I mean?"

I think I guessed that this time it was different, but saying no to Kenny was never easy, and downright impossible when I was in the mood myself, which I was just then.

"Sure, Ken." I rolled over and took hold of him. He was higher on the bed than I was, so his belly was right in front of my face. I could smell the sweet, musty smell of his thighs, mingled with the scent of soap. He'd showered, I decided, before coming to my room.

"Put your mouth on it," he said after a moment—not demanding, just asking in a quiet voice.

It gave me pause. We'd never done anything like that before, and I don't think I'd ever thought about it, favorably or otherwise. But Kenny had asked. Knowing him, he probably hadn't thought of it either before then, or he'd have mentioned it. Kenny wasn't shy about what he wanted.

I had never thought about a cock being beautiful before, or even especially desirable in itself. It was something to have fun with and take pleasure with. But now I was staring at Kenny's in a different way—and all of a sudden, it was beautiful. I stared at the head of it, mysteriously dark in the pale light, at the length of it, silky smooth and pale, with the faint color of veins running raggedly along it, like the marble on the dresser in Olsen's room that had fascinated me so much when I was little. The hair at the base was already

24

thick and glossy black. I could see his belly heaving up and down the way it did when he was excited.

I did what he'd asked, putting my lips lightly on the end of it. He let out his breath in a rush and moved slightly toward me.

"I like that," he said in a whisper. He put his hands on my head, mussing my hair with his fingers, and coaxed me gently downward. "That's nice."

I didn't know whether I liked it or not. It was strange tasting and kind of uncomfortable when it went into my throat. I choked on it and had to stop for a moment while he waited without moving, but I started in again and it got easier than it had been to begin with.

Of course Kenny was not about to be left out of anything new. "Let me try," he said after a bit. And as usual he couldn't go at it slowly and test the water. He had to swallow it all down like a starving man—and almost choked himself to death.

"Whew," he said, gasping for breath and coughing. "It's funny, isn't it?"

"I want to fuck you," I said on an impulse. That was the first time that idea had ever occurred to me, but now that the thought had come into my mind, I knew that I had wanted it that way for a long time.

"In the back?"

"Yes."

If he'd said no, I'd have let it go at that. I was already scared at my audacity to even suggest it. He was always the one that thought up new stuff for us to do. But he thought about it for a minute and then he said simply, "Okay."

Neither one of us knew how to go about it, and it took a while to figure out the right positions even. The two of us laughed a little, from nervousness and from our ignorance. But we got it figured out soon enough, and after a couple of bad tries, I got it started.

"Ouch," he said. He had been holding his breath, and he let it out loudly and jerked away from me.

"Hurt?" I asked, pausing. I knew it had, as tight as he had felt. Half of me wanted to stop, but the other half wanted badly to go on.

"No," he lied, and pushed back toward me. He wasn't likely to admit that he couldn't take it after he had agreed to it, and if I tried to stop now, he would have thought I considered him a baby.

I went on with it, taking it slow, trying to be gentle even though I was pretty clumsy at it. After a little, I could tell his reactions. I could feel him tense up each time I went a little deeper into him, and I would stop where I was, letting him get used to it. And when I felt him relax a little, I'd go on.

I had never been so excited over anything before, or so happy. It was more than just the physical pleasure of being in someone, although that was certainly thrilling enough. Kenny was giving himself to me, and I knew then, suddenly and beyond any question, that I loved him—loved the soft little cheeks brushing against my thighs as I pushed into him, loved the dark hair of his head that my face was buried in, loved the feel of my hand on his cock, hard still so that I knew what I was doing had not turned him off.

I think the little devil learned to like it. He started pushing it back to me after a while, and wriggling around. He kept getting harder and harder in my hand and then suddenly he stiffened and came, shooting over my hand and his belly and wetting the bedclothes. His body shook and convulsed the way it did when he came, and I made it a minute behind him, emptying myself far up inside him, hugging the breath from him. He took it all without a complaint and afterward he laughed and called me "Big Swede," but he didn't mean it the way he had before.

It never happened again. When my desire went, it was replaced by a river of guilt that suddenly separated me from him. I was ashamed of what we had done—of what I had done. It was wrong, I was sure of it, and crazy. We weren't kids anymore, we were men, and men didn't do things like this.

Kenny was puzzled at first, and later angry. He never did understand why I was upset. "What's wrong with it?" he wanted to know, arguing with me in tense whispers. "We both liked it, didn't we? I liked it better than with girls, Mar,

26

I really did. It's not like it was anybody else, it's you and me.
Hell, I'd do it again. Right now, if you want to.

"No." I jerked away from him when he tried to reach
for me. He would have done it again right then, I knew. He
was like that. One time just made him hungrier for the next.
"Let me alone."

I said it sharper than I meant to, and in a tone I had
never used with him before, and it hit home. Even without
looking at him, I knew I had hurt him. He didn't say anything after that.

"Go to bed," I said finally. I was tired all of a sudden,
and mixed up. And the worst of it was, I wanted it too, again,
but not badly enough.

Kenny didn't have any guilt of his own, I'm sure of
it, but some of mine rubbed off on him. The next day, it was
all different between us. He didn't look straight at me when
we were around each other, and we didn't say anything more
to each other than we had to. When I went to bed that night, I
saw him give me a funny looked. He wanted a sign, I know,
or some word that told him everything was okay, but I didn't
give him any. He came to bed later and stopped at my room,
opening the door and sticking his head inside.

"Mar," he said in a whisper, "You asleep?"

I wasn't, but a pretended I was. I never was a good
liar. He knew I was pretending, and that must have hurt most
of all. He waited a minute or two and then he went on to his
own room, and I spent the whole night staring up at the ceiling and wishing he were in bed with me, curled up in my
arms.

* * * * * *

That was the last time he ever came down to my
room at night. I came to hate myself for what I had done—
not for screwing around like we had, but for hurting him the
way I had, and shutting him out. I prayed for weeks that he
would try again and I knew if he did that I would say, "yes"
without any hesitation.

Right or wrong, good or bad, he had tormented my
every dream at night, and through the whole day I couldn't

think of anything but Kenny—loving him, wanting him. I was nearly crazy from it all. I tried everything I could think of to show him how I felt, that it was all right now. A hundred times I suggested we go for a hike in the woods, or go into town together, or wrestle in the barn. He wasn't having any, though. I had refused him once, something nobody had ever done before, and I wasn't to have a second chance.

The worst of it was that he wanted it too. He hadn't lied about liking what we had done. This was a whole new game for him and he wanted to play it to the hilt. But he was stubborn as an ox, and when he played again, it wasn't with me.

I suppose, in a sense, I was the one who drove him to Dexter Holloman. From that standpoint, I was the cause of the storm that brewed during those following months. When it broke finally, it was sudden and furious, and in the end it swept Kenny away from us.

Strange to say, though, I probably suffered the least when Kenny left, disappearing one day to remain gone for five long years. Not that I didn't miss him, in a way that none of the others could share, or even imagine; but for me, he had gone earlier.

He had left me after that night in my room. He had come back to Hanover, to the farm, but he had never come back to me.

CHAPTER THREE

It seemed that I had barely closed my eyes when Olsen tapped at my door to wake me. Homecoming or no homecoming, there was work to be done on a farm, even in October, and I had that to see to.

Usually we had the house to ourselves in the morning. There was always the aroma of fresh coffee from below as I cleaned up. It coaxed me along, hurrying me on my way. By the time I finally came down to the kitchen, Olsen would have our breakfast almost ready. There would be just time for me to wake up over the coffee before she set plates of ham and eggs and fresh bread in front of me, a small dish for herself; and then we would eat and talk, never anything too lengthy or serious. She kept up on how the farm was going, and I will give her credit, she knew as well as I did how much hay we would bring in this year, what prices it would fetch, which of the hands was earning his pay with good work and which ones wouldn't likely be kept on another year.

Sometimes, too, I would hear of how things were going in the house: Mrs. Baker's health, problems with the plumbing, whatever mattered in her world. It was a pleasant time of day. As mother and son, I suppose Olsen and I weren't any outstanding success, but I often thought that as partners we worked fine.

I had forgotten though that before he had gone, Kenny had always been there with us during these early

29

morning visits. If anything, he woke earlier than the two of us. It seemed almost as if he resented the time spent on sleeping, although I have never known a man who could fall asleep as quickly as he did, sleep as innocently untroubled, or wake as quickly.

He was there this morning, just the way it had been in the past. I heard his hearty laugh as I was coming down the stairs, too loud as usual, and sounding like he hadn't one care to his name.

"Pity the poor rabbits," I thought with a grin. "He's sure to be out after them today." The grin faded as I remembered that Kenny would be hunting something more serious than rabbits today.

I don't know when I had seen Olsen in such spirits. I'm sure she had not looked so young in a long while. Kenny had told some joke or funny story, and the two of them were rocking back and forth in their chairs, their shoulders shaking with laughter. They were eating already, I noticed. I must have been slower cleaning up than usual, I thought, and shrugged away the slight flash of resentment.

"Good morning," I greeted them, heading straight for the stove and the coffeepot. Olsen started to scramble up, but I shooed her back into her chair. "Sit. I'll get it," I said.

"You're up early," Kenny said behind me. "I figured you'd sleep till noon."

It was an odd thing for him to say, odd even allowing for the time that had gone by. He couldn't have forgotten all those mornings.

"My habits haven't changed much." I answered. I turned away from the stove and met his eyes, dark and intense upon me. He looked puzzled and, for just a moment, confused. But he came back with one of his "Fooled you, didn't I?" grins.

"Haven't they? You used to take sugar in your coffee and you're drinking that without any," he said.

He was right. It was a habit that I had changed, for no particular reason. But fast as his answer was, it didn't altogether satisfy. Something had begun to trouble me—nothing that I could put my finger on, but it was there like a vague ache in your teeth that you can't quite find with your tongue.

30

It came and went away and came back again during the days that followed, and with each return it had grown stronger, and more definite.

For the moment, however, there was nothing more than a quick note of discord and then things were all right again and I was relaxing at the table. Olsen got up and fixed my breakfast, all the while keeping up with the conversation. It was easy talk, relaxed and friendly, and it skirted around the questions with which we were all still occupied.

Kenny seemed to me more relaxed than he had been the night before. I found myself wondering how he had slept, what memories the sight of his room might have brought back to him. Had he, like I, remembered those nights when he had left his room and come to mine? But I pushed that thought back to where it had come from. It was one thing to remember, and even to be wishful, but I was not blind. However relaxed he might be, however friendly, it was plain that there was no intimacy between Kenny and me. He talked as he might talk to an acquaintance of the past, but there was nothing more, and I had to face that.

I finished breakfast and lingered longer than usual over coffee. Finally, when it was well past time when I should have been at work, I stood up, hesitating slightly. Knowing Kenny, he was not the sort to loaf around or remain inactive. Even if he were, he had plenty of reasons for being interested in the farm and how it was coming along.

"They've just finished with the hay," I said, concentrating my attention on the last sip of coffee in my cup. "I'm going out there now to see how it's going. Want to come along?"

As soon as I had said it, I realized that he couldn't come with me out to the fields, whether he wanted to or not. He was the son of the house by birth and by name, but it was a claim he had forfeited when he had gone, and it was a claim that right now was far from settled. His mother had yet to say whether he had any concern in how the farm was going or whether the hay was in.

"Thanks," he answered without any hesitation, like he had already thought all this out for himself. No doubt he had. "But I think I'll stay around the house today, kind of get the feel of things again. It's been a while."

I nodded and started for the door. "Does Pete still work the fields?" he asked after me.

I was glad he had asked after the old man. I think that one question did more than anything else to restore Kenny to the spot he had always held in my affection, and I was even smiling when I looked back at him.

"Not anymore," I said. "He looks after the equipment and does chores for Olsen. You'll probably find him in the barn if you go looking for him."

He seemed to understand the reason for my smile. He grinned back at me as though to say, "I want you to like me." For a brief moment the years had fallen away from us.

"I'll track him down later, maybe," he said.

"He'll want to talk with you. He must have a real store of yarns saved up by now."

I guess it sounded like I was criticizing him for having been gone, or at least reminding him of the fact. His grin faded, and our moment went with it.

"See you later," I finished lamely, and went out.

"See that you're back for dinner," Olsen called as the screen door banged shut after me.

I saw Pete myself, when I went to take the Jeep out of the barn. He was repairing a halter, and I found myself thinking that he must be repairing it for Kenny. We only had two horses now, Jezebel and Ladyship, and those two did little enough to earn their keep. No one rode them anymore and even if they had been suited for work, we had no need of them for that purpose. Jezebel could still be ridden, if she had a mind to let you, which was always in question, but Ladyship had a game leg, and it wouldn't have been worth the risk to her. Kenny had always liked to ride, though, even if he hadn't been very great at it, and he would probably be doing so, soon again. "I guess you're glad to see Kenny back," I said to Pete as I climbed into the Jeep and started it up.

If he was, he didn't show it. I suppose he was still sore over the greeting he had gotten. He continued to work at the halter, squinting to make up for his bad eyesight. "Has he seen her yet?" he asked. I knew who he meant, of course.

"Not yet." I backed out of the barn and turned the Jeep around in the yard. When I glanced up, Ingrid was standing at the window of her bedroom, staring out. She had been there the morning before, too. Then, she had been watching for Kenny to arrive. Now she was watching for…for what? I didn't know, any more than I could explain my own mood of things "going to happen."

There was that meeting, of course, between Kenny and his mother, and we were all waiting for that. But there was something more, something I couldn't understand but was sure the others felt too. The prodigal son had come home, the fatted calf had had her day on the table, but the electric atmosphere that had built up was still charging the air about the place with tension.

Ingrid saw me and waved, and disappeared from the window, and I drove off toward the back fields. I was luckier than most, I suppose—certainly luckier than Kenny, who faced a day of waiting around the house for something that might not even happen. At least I could keep busy and lose myself in hard physical work, as I had been doing for five years. Farm hands and farm managers don't as a rule need pills for their nerves, and today I was grateful for that fact.

The farm year was almost over for us, and the work nearly done. We had even had a frost earlier, a light one, before the weather turned hot. But I was too well acquainted with the fickle nature of our weather, to think that it would continue to favor us for long. We had started the fall work early, for no better reason than that Olsen had informed me one morning, while rubbing a bothersome elbow, that she felt cold weather coming, and I had learned long ago to trust her intuitions.

There was the winter planting yet to be done, and then the work would be light for the rest of the year. The farm encompassed more than two thousand acres, most of it in this one location, but with two smaller properties nearby as well. That was a big farm and a rich one, even by the standards of the area, which were high. That meant a lot of farming, especially in the spring and the fall, but we worked mostly summer crops and, with Pete and another man working regularly on the repairs and upkeep usually reserved for cold months, our winters were easy ones.

That had been a necessary schedule when I had been in school and there was no one to run the farm, and we had stuck with it since then. Others argued that the farm could turn twice the profit, and probably it could have, but we did well enough as it was. Another owner, one interested mostly in accumulating wealth, could have done very well indeed by the Baker lands. There was a large piece of land, mostly untended, that could be turned into a highly profitable place too. In addition to that, there was another small farm that had been rented out in the past and had produced a small but livable income for the farmer tenants. They had moved from there the year before, and Mrs. Baker had shown little interest in replacing them, so that, except for keeping the house and the farm buildings in repair, we did little or nothing with that.

Mrs. Baker was old, of course, and no one imagined that she would live too many more years. She had all the income from the property that she needed or would ever need. Someday soon it would pass into other hands—maybe Kenny's, maybe not. Whoever it was would be getting a lot, not a great fortune, maybe, but not a small one either.

I wondered if Kenny had thought much of that, and whether that had influenced his coming back. He had never given much thought to money when he was young, but a young man didn't, usually, not until he had gotten old enough to appreciate its value. At any rate, Kenny had never been poor, not so long as he had been at home. People who have never had money, and those who have always had it, don't as a rule attach much importance to it. It's those who've had it and lost it to whom it means the most.

I felt guilty harboring such thoughts, and yet I found myself again and again wondering how Kenny had lived since he had gone from here. How hard had he had to work to earn what kind of living? How many things had he wanted that he'd had to admit he couldn't afford and that there had suddenly been no one to afford for him?

Enough to make him think about the money in this land? Enough to cause him to remember that this could have belonged to him, and might yet? Enough—I tried not to think of this, but it came anyway, in the stubborn way that unpleasant thoughts have—enough to bring him home?

That was the question that was really bothering me, and now that I had faced it, it wouldn't go away, but kept hanging around in my head no matter how hard I tried to lose myself in my work.

What had brought Kenny home? His mother? I tried to remember what it had been like between the two of them, whether they had been close, whether they had loved one another in the way that some mothers and sons love one another—but I honestly didn't know. Somehow I had always thought of Kenny as loving everyone generally and no one specifically. Maybe that was because I had been afraid of realizing who and what he didn't love. He had never said to me, "Mar, I love you," and I guess for that reason I had never let myself imagine him saying it to anyone else.

But he had loved the farm. I couldn't deny that. For all his carelessness and his chasing after things, I had always believed in his love for this land. He had taken to the tractors and the farm equipment the way some young men take to women or drink. He had romanced the sun through many a summer, and there had been more honest passion in the way he threw hay than had been evident in any of his little episodes with the girls around town.

Maybe this was what had brought him home. Or maybe it was just the fact that this was home. Kenny was the sort who had to have someplace to go. Maybe he had come to the point during those five years where there was no place else to go but home.

I'd have given anything to have that question answered, but there was only one person who could have answered it, and I wasn't likely to put my question to him.

KENNY'S BACK, BY VICTOR J. BANIS

CHAPTER FOUR

If all the pieces to the peaceful picture of Kenny's return had not yet been fitted into place, there was one piece that stood out the most in my mind: Dexter Holloman. I don't know what the others expected to take place in that respect. For all I knew, Kenny himself might not yet know whether he would see Dexter. But I knew, in a way that none of them could have known.

Oddly enough, although he lived only a little more than a mile up the road, I scarcely knew Dexter. Certainly I knew little enough how he felt, or what after this time he might feel for Kenny.

But I knew Kenny. I knew what it was like to love him and, for all his faults, Dexter must have loved him to some degree. I knew the sort of things that Kenny could do to you once you had learned to love him, too, things that were never quite undone. You might learn to live with it, you might send him away to some dark corner of your mind where you almost but not quite forgot that he was there—but he came back, just as he had done in real life. He called you out of your sleep, even, and you came, and were glad to do so.

I knew that if I had been Dexter Holloman—if I had been Kenny's lover, as Dexter tragically had been, if I knew that he were back, as Dexter must know by now—somehow, some way, damn any consequences, I would see Kenny.

Kenny's lover. I'll probably never know just how accurate that term was, how much or how little they had really cared for one another. I knew, and most everyone in Hanover knew, that there had been a "relationship," as some of the more polite townspeople called it. But in truth none of us knew very much about what actually went on, or why.

On Kenny's part, I suppose some of it may have been spite aimed at me because I had turned him down. And a big part of it was nothing more than curiosity, and the fact that he had discovered a new kind of excitement. I've always believed that had that relationship been allowed to run its natural course, it would have died out soon enough, and all our lives would have been different.

It was stupid of me to have simply told Kenny no. I can see that now. I should have known that he would never buy that answer. What I had refused him, he was sure to get elsewhere, even if only to prove that he could.

By all rights, he should have been unsuccessful at it. Hanover wasn't big enough, or wild enough, to offer much of that sort of thing. It went on, I suppose, mostly among kids, the same as with us, but for all that he was friendly with people, Kenny had been something of a loner most of his life. He had a few friends, and his girlfriends and such, but I doubt that he was close to anyone, except for me. And this wasn't the sort of thing you could try with someone you only knew slightly—unless it was someone like Dexter.

Dexter wasn't a Hanover man, or a Hanover type, and although he lived in the country, he wasn't even a farmer. He met and married Edna Hill in Chicago and came back to Hanover with her. For all I know, maybe he loved her, or maybe it was the fact that Edna's family were comfortably well off and he could look forward to a life as a country gentleman.

If it was the money that attracted him to the small-town girl and the small-town life, his luck ran well. Soon after the newlyweds were installed in the house up the road, Edna's parents were killed in a crash, and his wife's fortune increased considerably.

Holloman was probably living better now than he had ever lived, at least as far as income went. It couldn't have been a very happy life for him, though. The stories had it that he had been a pretty wild type in Chicago, and there were gossips enough that his little adventures had not exactly ended when he came to Hanover.

Maybe that wasn't entirely his fault. Edna had never been a healthy girl and most folks had thought of her as a little odd herself. Anyway, after her parents died, she seemed to be sick more often than not. She grew thin and pale and weak looking, and although she wasn't seen in town much, the people who did see her from time to time said she acted downright crazy.

There was a bit of ugliness the year before Kenny left that should have given us fair warning. Dexter was accused by a kid from another town nearby of having tried to "fool around." At the time, it was all quieted down quickly and without much fuss, and there might even have been some money involved in settling the matter, although that's nothing more than a guess.

At any rate, according to the stories, Dexter's wife grew crazier than ever for a while after that, and some said she had tried to divorce him. Dexter was no fool, however. He was next in line for a sizable estate, and the wife who controlled it now was in failing health, mentally and physically. If he could hold on to her for a while, a few years, there was more than an even chance that he would be her heir. If things got too difficult, as they might have during that period, there was always the question of her sanity, and he made it plain, to her and to the local gossips, that he was not above using that as a weapon. He went so far as to send Edna away to a "rest home," where she stayed three months, until the doctors decided she was well enough to come home.

Needless to say, she was more subdued after that. I don't think for a moment she was cured of any insanity, if she was suffering from insanity to begin with, but her hand had been slapped, and she had been warned what was in store for her if she tried to do Dexter out of his new wealth.

It looked as though Dexter had played the winning cards and had taken the game—and up to that point, he had, but he had reckoned without two factors. One of them was the temperament of a woman who had been spoiled rotten

39

most of her life and was using to winning by fair means or foul. The other was Kenny.

No one knows just how it began between them. Dexter being what he was, and living so near, he had undoubtedly seen Kenny many times, and more than likely he had wanted what he saw, but without thinking that there was any likelihood of having it.

Somehow, though, somewhere, they met again, and now Dexter suddenly realized, either by instinct or because Kenny made it plain to him, that the opportunity was ripe. Dexter seized it quickly. He had himself a new toy, to play with a bit and then forget, and Kenny had found the means of continuing the new adventure he had discovered with me.

A man playing the sort of games Dexter was playing cannot afford to be careless, but he was. Somehow, Edna discovered what was going on. If hers had been an ordinary marriage, she might have handled it all different. If she had loved Dexter enough, she might have forgiven him and waited it out, waited for the newness to wear off and her husband to come back to her. But Edna wanted out, she wanted to divorce her husband, and to do that, she needed powerful ammunition, powerful enough to call his hand if he tried to send her away again.

Kenny had given her that kind of ammunition and she saw to it that it did not slip out of her fingers. Chances were she deliberately made it easy for them, staying out of their way until the time was ripe. She waited, stringing out the line, until they had time to become careless.

They met on Dexter's property, as we learned later. At one time it had been a bigger place than it was now. When Edna's grandparents had lived there, it had been more of an estate than a farm and, set off from the farmhouse itself, secluded by a grove of trees, was a small house that had been the caretakers. It had long since been empty and had fallen into such an advanced state of disrepair that it would have taken more to put it into livable shape than the building was worth. As a meeting place for lovers, though, it was quite satisfactory, and it was here that Kenny and Dexter had conducted their relationship.

When Edna decided at last that it was time to act, she called Mrs. Baker. From what I heard of the conversation and from Mrs. Baker's comments, Edna must have sounded every bit as crazy as people said she was. Despite that fact, though, there must have been a ring of sincerity to her pleas that Mrs. Baker come at once. Edna offered no explanation except that it was about Kenny, who was out that evening. Mrs. Baker thought, I'm sure, that Kenny had been up to some new mischief, but the call had made it sound as though this was especially serious, and she asked me to go with her and drive her to the Holloman place.

I nearly created a greater tragedy. We had just reached the lane that led to Holloman's house, and as I started to turn from the road, a figure appeared in front of the car, seemingly from nowhere. The car skidded on gravel as I swerved sharply and we slid into the grass of the ditch as Edna ran up to the window of the car. She was wild-eyed and beside herself with excitement.

"Here," she said in a hoarse voice, "This way."

I thought we were going to the house, and I was none too happy with the fact that she had nearly caused us to wreck the car. "Wait," I told her, "I'll get the car out."

"No, leave it here." She opened the car door and practically dragged Mrs. Baker out of the car. Mrs. Baker looked more alarmed by Edna's appearance than any thought of Kenny, but we seemed to have no choice but to follow Edna as she ran into the trees. She avoided the driveway and instead led us along a well-worn but overgrown path, to the old caretaker's house, silencing us with a determined gesture when we tried to question her.

The ramshackle cottage, almost hidden among the trees, seemed to be dark within until we were almost to it, and then we saw the faint glow of a light from behind boarded up windows.

"Quiet, don't let them know we're coming," Edna whispered frantically as we drew near. It was eerie, the three of us stealing through the darkness, Mrs. Baker and I with no idea what we were after. We reached the house and I saw Mrs. Baker hesitate, and I don't think I would have minded if she had asked me right then to take her home, but she squared her shoulders and followed Edna to the door. Edna's hand paused as she reached for the door and then, with a flourish, she threw it open.

If only they had finished the act itself—but they had not. They were in the first room, just inside the door. There were no furnishing except a battered table on which stood a lantern, and a large old bed that had been fitted out with clean sheets.

Dexter and Kenny were on the bed, stark naked. They were wound together, sixty-nining, so wrapped up in what they were doing, they were completely unaware of us.

It was like coming upon a murder scene. I froze. I didn't know what to do, and for a moment we only stood and watched. Dexter obviously reached his climax as we stared, and there was actually the sight of semen spilling from the corners of Kenny's mouth. Worst of all were the blissful expressions on both faces.

It was a horrible scene for us to witness like this. Edna had played her trump card, and her anxiety released itself now in hysterical laughter that finally announced our presence to the two men on the bed. They sprang apart, staring wide-eyed at us.

My first thought was for Mrs. Baker. Stunned, she let me pull her back out of the house. "I don't...." She tried to say something but I hurried her back along the path as fast as I could.

"Wait in the car," I told her, giving her orders as though I were the boss and she the hired hand. "I'll straighten it all out."

I knew that soon enough she would recover from the initial shock and then she would take control again, but I was trying to make it as easy as possible for her—and for Kenny.

I left her in sight of the car and ran as fast as I could back to the cottage. Edna's laughter was still ringing in my ears, but it was only a memory. She wasn't laughing now, she was screaming, and trying to get away from an enraged Dexter, who was beating her savagely. Kenny, half in, half out of his clothes, was trying without much success to separate them and cover himself at the same time.

Getting them apart was a chore. While I struggled with them, Kenny found the rest of his clothes and got into them. I still had my hands full when he had finished. I had never seen him look so stunned. His face was as white as fresh snow, his eyes large and black. The one look he gave me as he ran out was more painful to me than anything I can remember in my life. I think that in that moment he hated me and blamed me for the intrusion.

I wanted to run after him, to cry with him and tell him that he need never have turned to someone like Dexter—but I still had my hands full with Dexter, trying to keep him off his wife, and Kenny went by me fast, out of the house and into the night.

For a brief moment I was alone with Dexter and his wife. I took advantage of the opportunity to offer the only comment I ever gave Dexter on his actions. He saw it coming, and he knew from my face what I was going to do. If he had any intelligence, he must have guessed too why I was doing it. That may have been why he didn't try to duck. Maybe he knew that he had it coming.

I hit him hard. A few years on a farm does more for an arm than a lifetime of lifting weights in a gym. Holloman seemed to draw up and then he lifted from the floor and went crashing across the room. I left them there, her crying into her hands, him out cold.

If the entire business had been kept quiet, it would have been bad enough, but it wasn't long to remain our secret. By the time Edna and Dexter had finished dragging one another in and out of courts, the story was not only public knowledge but considerably more lurid than it had been to start with, which was bad enough.

Edna went for a divorce, and Dexter was just as quick to demand that she be committed as insane, and neither one missed any chance at flinging dirt. A great deal of the dirt had Kenny's name attached to it. Some of it dirtied the rest of us, too—Mrs. Baker and I were both forced to testify to what we had seen, not once but multiple times.

Chances are Edna would have won ultimately—she had the honors of the field, after all—but her triumph had done more than all Dexter's conniving to unseat her mind, and she did more than Dexter could ever have done to prove her lack of sanity. The tide seemed briefly to be going in Dexter's favor, and the thought that she might lose after fighting so hard was more than Edna's weak mind could bear.

It may have been that she intended Dexter to be accused of murdering her, and there was for a time some question as to whether her death really was suicide, but if it was anything else, Dexter was not her murderer. Unknown to her, he was a hundred miles away at the time and in conference with two doctors whose reputations were too great to even suspect them of perjuring themselves.

In the end, Dexter won after all. He was still her husband when she died and, as a result, her heir. There were no close relatives to contest the will, only a couple of distant cousins, and no one took their claims very seriously.

His victory, as it turned out, was not all it might have seemed. The estate when it was finally settled and the attorneys' fees paid, was considerably smaller than most guesses at its size had been. Once he had full control over it, it was to dwindle even more, until by now it was no secret that he had begun to suffer money problems.

Kenny was lucky in one respect, at least. All of this went on after he was gone and he was spared the sort of humiliation that he would certainly have suffered otherwise; but he had suffered quite a lot as it was. He had been degraded and shamed, in front of his mother and me. And we made it worse. I realized that later.

He was home when we got back that night. He had never run away from taking his medicine before, and I admired him for not doing so this time. Olsen told me later that he had come in looking like a wild man, and even Ingrid, who was standing in the hall when we arrived, looked frightened and bewildered. She was just a kid then, but old enough to know that something had taken place. She searched our faces for some explanation, but of course neither of us offered any.

Later, when it was obvious that the story was out, Mrs. Baker gave Olsen a brief explanation of what had really happened, and I added to it slightly. To Olsen's credit, she never asked, nor do I believe that she ever listened or credited any of the increasingly lurid tales that circulated about town.

"Where's Kenny?" Mrs. Baker asked Ingrid as she came in that night. Her voice was hard and cold. It was the first she had spoken since we had left the Holloman's.

"In there," Ingrid told her in a tiny voice, pointing to the closed door of the parlor

I witnessed only a little of that scene, and that only because I was supporting Mrs. Baker and helped her into the parlor. Kenny looked at me first, rather than his mother. He was no longer angry or accusing. It was more as though he were asking me to understand.

If I could go back and change any part of that whole business, it would be one tiny detail: the way I looked back at him. I was angry by now, furiously angry. Angry with Dexter, angry with Kenny, angry with myself for the part I had played in it all. And I was more hurt and jealous than I realized at the time. I shot back a look at him that must have withered his last hope for an ally, someone to whom he could turn for consolation. For perhaps the first time in his life, he was truly on his own.

His mother had forgiven a lot in the past, although when she was aroused she had a temper to match Kenny's. She was aroused now, and this time it was not some boyish prank or harmless mischief that Kenny had done, but something that went against her entire moral fiber and her religious passion. She raised the kind of hell Kenny had never been subject to before. I think I was more shocked by the heat of her anger than I had been by Kenny's acts.

At first he took it well, maybe hoping that it would lessen finally and that he could again charm his way back into favor—but it got worse, and it was Mrs. Baker's turn to make mistakes. She did the one thing that was sure to spell disaster: she ordered Kenny. She set down her demands in no uncertain terms and with no room for argument. Kenny would humble himself, not just before us, but before most of the town. He would go to church the following Sunday, and when the minister made his usual call for repentant sinners, Kenny would go to the altar and beg forgiveness for his sins.

Furthermore, he was forbidden to ever see, or even go near, Dexter. He would not, in fact, leave the property at all except in the company of one of us. In short, not only was he to humiliate himself publicly, but privately as well, by becoming virtually our prisoner.

I could have argued for him. Even as angry as I was, I knew that Kenny would never do as his mother demanded, regardless of what his refusal might cost him. He had too much pride, and too much stubborn temper that flared up sometimes before he thought.

I didn't, though. I didn't say a word. I looked at him, standing with his shoulders perfectly straight and with tears in his eyes that might have been from hurt, shame or anger— and I left the room, closing the door on them. This was their quarrel, I convinced myself, and none of my business. I was only a hired hand. As I went out, I glanced again at Kenny and I saw at once how fully I had failed him, and how much it mattered to him; but the door was already closing, and I let it.

That was the last I saw of him until five years later. I don't know what else was said that night, what threats and warnings and demands were hurled back and forth. From the kitchen I heard the door crash open and Kenny run up the stairs to his room. Olsen gave me a dreadful look and hurried to Mrs. Baker. Ingrid, who had waited silently in the kitchen with us, ignorance making it even worse for her, started crying quietly into her hands.

I went out to the barn and tired to busy myself with unnecessary chores there—and tried not think of the young man that I knew by this time I loved.

* * * * * * *

Olsen was alone in the kitchen when I came down the following morning. "Kenny's gone," was the first thing she said to me.

"Gone where?" I asked stupidly.

"Gone," she repeated, and when I looked at her face, I knew just what she meant.

46

It wasn't hard to guess that Mrs. Baker tried to find him. There were phone calls all over the country, all hours of the day and night, and letters from cities and towns I had never heard of, not to mention a regular parade of strangers who came and went from the house, spending their time there closed in her rooms with her.

She may have found him, at least determined his whereabouts and that he was all right, but if she did no one but she and possibly Olsen, who spent a lot of her time now caring for the widow, knew about it. I myself did not hear anything more until, after five empty years had gone by, the letter came.

When it came, it was for Ingrid, a fact that might have explained some of the coolness that I felt toward Kenny. I didn't even see it, in fact, although she read it to Olsen and me, and to Mrs. Baker, too. Olsen wanted to take it herself to the mother, but Ingrid was having too much fun being the center of attention, and she held out until she was allowed to take the letter to Mrs. Baker's rooms and read it herself.

It didn't say much, only that Kenny was in Indiana, and that he would like to come home for a visit if that was all right.

I was hurt that Kenny had written to Ingrid instead of me, but I was even more surprised that he had not written directly to his mother. He had never been one to ask someone else to do his work for him. But that was only a minor detail, and I would be a fool to say that I was any less excited about the prospect of his return than anyone else.

Of all of us, Mrs. Baker took it the most calmly. Olsen had seriously feared what the news might do to the heart that had already grown dangerously weak, and it was for this reason that she had wanted to break the news herself. She contented herself, however, by preparing Mrs. Baker for a letter from her son.

In fact, from what Olsen and Ingrid told me afterward, Mrs. Baker seemed neither surprised nor excited. Ingrid was even doubtful whether the aging woman had actually heard the letter, and was on the verge of reading it again, when Mrs. Baker finally commented on it.

"Will you be writing him?" she asked, speaking directly to Ingrid.

"Yes, I—I guess so," Ingrid managed to stammer when she had gotten over her surprise at the question.

"Ask him when he'll be coming."

That was the way it was left. Permission had not been given directly, but it had at least been implied, and in a few days we had the reply from Kenny, giving us the date of his arrival. From the day of that letter on, I doubt that any of us thought of anything except that Kenny was coming home.

He was still miles away, yet already he had begun again to dominate our lives and our thoughts.

CHAPTER FIVE

I was late coming back into the house. The sun had already made its climb upward and was now on its way back down to the horizon. I knew Olsen would be hopping if I made her meal late, and I drove the Jeep faster than usual along the dirt track that crossed the pasture.

I realized something was up as soon as I came in sight of the barn. Pete was just leading the horses from the barn into the makeshift corral we had built behind it. That meant that either dinner was over already, or it was going to be considerably late. Either was unusual.

My guess would have been that something had happened at the house, something important enough to upset Olsen's rigid schedules. But as I turned into the yard, I saw Kenny and Ingrid come around the house. They were playing like a pair of young colts, him chasing her and catching her as she reached the yard. From the fact that they were outside, and the carefree way they were laughing and cutting up, I knew that nothing too drastic had taken place yet.

They saw me and waved. For a moment I felt a pang of jealousy. They looked happier than I would have expected—the way I would like to have felt, I reminded myself, and then I became angry at myself for being so childish. Why shouldn't they be happy and enjoying one another's company, I asked myself? They were both still young, not much more than kids, and they were the sort to laugh and play games. It wasn't their fault if I was overly solemn and stuffy, and in bad spirits because the field work was going slower than I would have liked.

I waved back and parked the Jeep in the shade of the barn. I remembered something I wanted to tell Pete, and went around the barn, toward the corral. He was seated atop the board fence, watching the two horses.

"Dinner's late," Pete greeted me, making it plain what matters most occupied his mind. "Olsen's busy somewhere."

To myself, I thought, Ingrid could have been inside taking care of the meal—but I didn't voice this opinion aloud. Running the house was Olsen's affair, and even though I thought she pampered Ingrid too much, I made it a point to keep that thought mostly to myself.

I had just finished with what I had come to talk over with Pete when Ingrid and Kenny joined us. They came around the barn laughing and holding hands. We heard them before they came into sight, their voices attracting even Jezebel's attention. The mare looked in their direction with mild curiosity.

"What's keeping dinner?" I asked of Ingrid as they came up to where we were standing. I wasn't in the best of humors, for a number of reasons, and it must have put an edge on my voice. Ingrid shot me a surprised look, but she was in too high spirits to be annoyed in return.

"Mrs. Baker wanted to see her," she said. "Olsen's been with her for an hour or so." She did not comment on the significance of this fact, but it was apparent. I saw, when I looked in Kenny's direction, that he was not quite as carefree as he had seemed either. I knew he realized what was coming and that he was trying hard to hide his anxiety.

"How's the work coming?" he asked me in a more sober mood.

"Fine," I answered curtly. I had never been able to keep up with Kenny's changes of mood. If I was feeling glum, I stayed glum for a while, and if I was happy it took a lot to change that, too. But Kenny could go through a dozen different frames of mind while I was just working myself out of one.

"Maybe tomorrow I'll ride out and look things over," he suggested.

"I have to go into town tomorrow. I'll need the Jeep," I said. I was being a little childish, I suppose. The trip to town could as easily have been put off a day, but Kenny's show of interest struck me as a piece of candy being offered to a difficult child, and right at the moment I wasn't interested in sweets.

He shrugged and I was a little sorry I had been so abrupt. Jezebel had cautiously moved a little closer, and she whinnied now to remind us of her presence.

"You could ride Jezebel out tomorrow," I said on an impulse. "You haven't forgotten her, have you?"

"Jezebel?" He looked surprised at the suggestion and turned his attention to the pen, looking first at Jezebel and then at Ladyship, who had noticed the attention the older mare was getting and was hurrying now to join us. I grinned slightly as I watched Kenny's face. Pete and I weren't the only ones to suffer from Kenny's memory, it seemed. He wasn't sure which horse was Jezebel, either.

"Of course she's gotten a bit old. She didn't have all that gray before," Ingrid said. She climbed up on one of the boards and reached across to pat Jezebel's mane. "But she's still a beauty. Remember how you used to ride the devil out of her, Ken?"

"I almost had forgotten," he said. He reached for Jezebel, but all of a sudden some of her mean spirit showed itself. She ducked and nipped at his hand.

"Looks like she hasn't forgotten," I commented. Kenny had jerked his hand back fast, startled by the mare's sudden move. I looked from the horse to him, and realized to my surprise that, for just a quick moment, he looked scared. That was something I had never seen before, and something I would never have expected to see in Kenny. He had never been a great horseman, but he had never been frightened by horses either.

He caught my look and I found myself gazing into those dark eyes. He must have guessed what I was thinking. "I haven't been close to a horse in five years," he said, looking straight back at me. "You lose the knack."

51

I was the one to back down. I had never been much for staring matches and I looked away now. Pete was staring too, not at me, but at Kenny. His eyes were squinted the way they were when he was trying to see something close despite his bad eyesight. I wondered fleetingly what it was he was trying to see in the familiar face. Then I turned away and started for the house.

"Better stay away from Jezebel, then," I said to Kenny as I started off. "In case you've forgotten, she was the mean one."

Kenny didn't follow me right away, but Ingrid did. She caught up with me halfway across the yard, almost running to keep up with my long stride.

"That was pretty cutting," she said sharply. "He doesn't have to be reminded that he's been gone."

"It seems to me that Kenny has to be reminded of quite a bit," I answered. "Maybe one of us had better describe his Mother to him, just in case he doesn't remember her too well. It might save some embarrassment."

"Mar!" She stopped, shocked by my remark. I went on in, letting the door bang after me.

Once I was inside, though, and by myself, I was a little ashamed. It had been a pretty mean thing to say, and the truth was, I wasn't being very friendly with Kenny. Strangest of all, I did not know just why I had the attitude I had. I was jealous, and hurt by the changes in him, of course, but I was glad to have him back, even if I was only a hired hand to him now.

Yet there was something that was rubbing me wrong, something that got my goat every time I was around him. If he paid me no attention, I sulked and felt left out. If he tried to be friendly, as he had done outside, I drew away from him and gave him a cold shoulder. I didn't know just what it was that I did want from him anymore.

"You're a son-of-a-bitch," I told myself in a quiet voice as I entered the kitchen. Sour grapes don't make for good eating.

Olsen was there in the kitchen by this time, working furiously to get her already late meal prepared. She turned from the stove, her face flushed.

"Did you say something to me?" she asked, pushing a strand of hair back from her forehead.

"Just talking to myself," I said. "How is she?" I nodded in the direction of Mrs. Baker's rooms.

"Yes, how is she?" It was Ingrid who repeated the question. She and Kenny had come in the back door just then. Ingrid gave me a frosty look and Kenny avoided looking at me altogether. It was easy to see, I wasn't winning any medals for popularity today.

Olsen set her spoon aside and wiped her hands on her apron. It was to Kenny that she spoke, and she was obviously excited. "She's up and dressed," she said. "I think she's going to see you today, Kenny. I'm sure of it. I had to help her get out of bed and she insisted on wearing one special dress, that blue one you gave her for her birthday the year…the last time you were here."

"Did she seem…?" Kenny hesitated, for once not sure of the word he wanted to use, and fumbling in a way that was new to him. "Was she excited?"

"Like a kid at Christmas," Olsen said. "She tried not to show it, but it couldn't be hidden. I only hope the excitement's not too much. She's very frail, Kenny."

"Maybe I should," he started to say, but he never finished what it was he thought he should do. My back was to the hall door, but I knew from the expressions on the faces of the others who had come into the room. I turned as though a gun had been fired.

Mrs. Baker had been, in her younger years, a woman of commanding appearance. She was short, like Kenny, but she had held herself and walked like she was taller, and there had been something regal about her that demanded the attention and the respect of others. As her health had slipped away from her, she had come to walk very little, and when she did, she no longer had the strength to hold herself in the old, erect manner.

Somehow, though, she had found the strength today. For a moment, in the first glimpse, she looked as young and as strong as I remembered her from the past.

Strangely, it was Olsen to whom she had turned first as she entered the room. "Olsen," she said, "I wonder if it would be too much trouble if we ate in the dining room. It will be cooler there, I think."

She wanted to show, I am sure, that it was still she who ran the house, lest there be any doubts on that score. And perhaps it was partially vanity, the desire of a woman to show that she was still her own mistress, that time had not troubled her overmuch. I suppose most of all she wanted to be the woman her son remembered.

She turned to Kenny then, looking directly at him for the first time in five years, and the mask that she had assumed so bravely crumbled. She managed to say his name, "Kenny," but that was all. No doubt she had planned what she wanted to say to him. From the time he had arrived she must have prepared and rehearsed whatever speech she had intended, but now it would not pass through her trembling lips. And with that evidence of her weakness and her emotion, her strength fled. She swayed and started to fall.

I was closest to her. Kenny was behind me, and clear across the room, but he beat me to her. He must have crossed the kitchen in one leap, and before I even fully grasped what had happened, he had her in his arms, supporting her frail body against his, and she was crying softly against his chest.

They had forgiven one another for the bitterness and the harsh words they had used when last they had seen one another. And, just then, watching with pride and emotion as Kenny led his mother back toward her room, whispering softly to her words not meant for the rest of us to hear, I forgave him too.

He was like that. He wouldn't let you stay mad at him. If ever the door was opened, you could never again entirely shut him out of your affections. I must have lied to myself when I said that I didn't know what I wanted from him. I knew.

Yes, damn it, I knew, even though I was just as sure that it would never be mine.

CHAPTER SIX

The question that we had all been waiting for had been asked and answered. Kenny's acceptance back into the fold was complete, or very nearly so, and it seemed clear now that he would be staying.

I never lost the feeling, though, that we were still waiting for something to happen. If it had been only my instinct, I would have credited it to my knowledge that sooner or later Kenny and Dexter would meet again, and to my concern about what that meeting would set off.

It wasn't just me, though. I was sure of it. Most of the time the others seemed fine, happy with the way things had worked out, and gradually settling back into a life that nearly belied Kenny's long absence.

There were other times, however, brief moments, in which it seemed they confirmed my apprehension. I would turn to catch a glimpse of Kenny, preoccupied with something that must have bothered him greatly, and his face would be sober, his forehead wrinkled in thought. Then he would see me, and the face would go instantly blank, or he would grin with such conviction that you almost doubted you had seen him worried. He was worried, though. I knew it—but about what?

Ingrid convinced me that I was right in my suspicions. She too had caught the scent of something awry, although like Kenny she tried hard to conceal her feelings. I would be talking to Kenny, never about anything very im-

portant—we didn't talk about important things anymore—
and I would suddenly know that someone was watching us.
Invariably, I would find it to be Ingrid, staring at us as
though trying to fathom what it was she was seeing.

In time I came to realize that it wasn't "us" she was
watching. At first, I thought she must somehow have known
what had happened between Kenny and me in the past, and
was on alert for any sign of something starting again.

Eventually, though, I realized that she was watching
Kenny, and that I was just coincidentally there. She watched
him almost constantly. If she was not with him, she was
never far away, and there was something frightened, and
frightening, in her watchfulness.

Odd, that though I had lived with Ingrid all of her
life, we had never shared the closeness that some brothers
and sister have. In many ways, we were strangers to one another. That was probably more my fault than hers. I wasn't
by nature an affectionate person, or a particularly open one
about my feelings. As a kid, I'd had to assume early on the
role of the man of the family. I had never minded it particularly, but it meant that when she and I might have been playing children's games together, I was working in the fields,
and when I should have been an older brother to her, I was
being farm boss to a bunch of hands. It was all right for me.
With one or two notable exceptions, I was content with my
life and the way it had gone. For her, it must have been a
lonely life, or at best an unexciting one.

We had moved around a lot before we had come to
the Baker house. As a little girl, Ingrid had not had much of a
chance to get acquainted with any of our homes, let alone
have any girl friends. We were poor, which didn't help much
either, and Ingrid, besides being a little spoiled, developed a
proud streak that formed a gulf between her and other girls
her age.

I remember that, even when she was a little girl, everyone always thought she was pretty, and of course, as it
turned out, they had been right. I guess I got the muscles of
the family and the full ration of practicality, and Ingrid had
gotten everything else: all the looks and the wit and the

56

charm—and the frustration that goes with not being able to use them the way they should be used.

She always dreamed of being someone. One time she would announce that she had decided to be a President's wife, and it only remained for her to select a President to her taste. A week later, she was set on being a great movie star and we would be treated to examples of her haughty grandeur and posing. When dancing became her guiding light, she never entered a room without twirling and spinning and bowing gratefully to our approving smiles.

I felt rather sorry for her, to think that she had succeeded in being nothing more than a farm girl. A year before, she had decided that, without any possibility of doubt, she was destined to be an artist. She had even selected a school she wanted to attend in the neighboring state. It was better than a hundred miles to Indianapolis and the school, and the tuition was expensive, but I had done what I could to help persuade Olsen to let her go.

"She deserves a little something," I expressed my opinion to Olsen, "Something more than what she has got here, which isn't much."

So off to school Ingrid had gone. Of course, that hadn't worked out any better than her other schemes. For a time, I thought it had. The first few months her letters were full of excitement and enthusiasm. She seemed to have found whatever it was she had been looking for. I thought it was the school. Olsen thought differently.

"She's in love," Olsen informed me one weekend when Ingrid was home, but not in the room with us. "She's met someone, Mar."

At first I wouldn't even admit the possibility. So far as I could see, Ingrid was still just a child, much too young for romance and the like. But of course, she wasn't, and after a time I began to think maybe Olsen was right. Ingrid had changed during her time away from home. She had ceased being a girl and had become a woman. There was a new flush to her cheeks, and her eyes sparkled with suppressed excitement. She had the sort of enthusiasm she hadn't displayed since her passion for dancing had burned out. Something, or someone, had excited her all right, and had given her the one thing she had lacked before: a purpose.

She never mentioned him, however; not a word. Whoever he was, this mysterious lover, I didn't exactly envy the poor fellow. He was getting a lot of temper and extravagance and childish nonsense. Aside from pitying him, though, I was secretly glad for her—and I was puzzled and disappointed when it seemed to fall through.

For a time it went along with apparent success. Ingrid was finding more and more excuses not to come home for weekends, and when she was home, her spirits were at fever pitch.

Then, all of a sudden, she was home to stay. Her explanation was simple: she had been unhappy with school. She said nothing about any romance and ignored the hints Olsen sometimes threw her way. I didn't see any signs of a broken heart. Except that she was more thoughtful now, and occasionally out of sorts, Ingrid didn't seem to suffer any from her romantic adventure. If romantic adventure there had been. Maybe Olsen had been wrong, though that was not often the case.

It may have been that Kenny's arrival came in time to offset any unhappiness she might have suffered, as it was only a month or so after her return that he wrote to us—or, rather, wrote to her. In any event, she was as preoccupied with him now as she had previously been with her unknown suitor. I was beginning to think our little Ingrid was not only a schemer, but fickle as well.

I waited. Kenny worried. Ingrid watched. It was a strange period. Yet these were only undercurrents, and though they were there and made their presence known in numerous little ways, they did not much mar the otherwise tranquil surface of our lives. I suppose if any of us had been asked to describe in one word that period of time, we would have said "quiet." For the most part, it was a happy period for the people sharing the house. The exceptions, I think, were largely in my feelings.

The changes in Kenny were even more pronounced since he had been accepted back into the fold. He was docile and sedate now. He spent more time about the house in the next week or so than he would have done in a year previously. There could be little doubt that he was glad his mother had forgiven him, and he seemed determined to make up for the affection and attention of which he had cheated her.

As for Mrs. Baker, Kenny's return to grace had proved to be a stronger medicine than any that her doctors had prescribed during the last few years. For almost a year she had lived as a recluse in her own rooms on the first floor. During that time, I had seen her just once a month, when I would report to her on the work, get her decisions and instructions, and make suggestions which usually she agreed to without much discussion. Once or twice it had even been necessary to forego our business meeting because her strength was not equal to it.

The change that had taken place with the return of her son was startling. That first meeting had been a strain on her, and Olsen grimly predicted a real setback as a result of the excitement, but instead she had recovered, and for a time she was no longer a recluse. She made herself as much as possible a part of the day-to-day routine of the house. She had her breakfast in her room, but she took the rest of her meals with us and spent most of her evenings and afternoons in the kitchen with Olsen and, more often than not, Kenny. Sometimes she would ask Kenny to help her out to the big front porch, and they would sit together for much of an afternoon on the porch swing, talking, or sometimes just sharing the quiet together.

Olsen had to scold and threaten bodily violence in order to persuade her to rest as she should, and even then it was only begrudgingly that Mrs. Baker allowed herself to be escorted back to her rooms for her periods of rest. Finally, Olsen had to appeal to the rest of us, and particularly to Kenny.

"She's running on borrowed strength," Olsen warned him solemnly. "Of course she wants to be out here, she wants to spend every possible minute near you. But the excitement and the effort could be too much for her if she doesn't take care of herself."

"She looks strong," Ingrid said. "I think she should be allowed to do as she wishes."

"I'm only saying what the doctors have told me time and time again," Olsen argued. "I'm not saying, Kenny, that she's going to die tomorrow. With proper care, they say she could live another ten, fifteen years. But something *could* happen, today, tomorrow, anytime."

"Maybe she is right, Ken," Ingrid relented. I was surprised at the interest Ingrid took in the subject, and surprised too that she, who had never given or taken advice in the past, should put herself now in the role of Kenny's advisor. But this time, at least, her advice was right, and I was glad that Kenny agreed.

"I'll help," he told Olsen. "We'll all of us try to keep her from getting excited or overdoing things, and we'll see that she gets her rest."

"Well, there's one thing to be grateful for," Ingrid commented. "At least she won't have all those lawyers visiting and wearing her out now."

All of us looked at her. Olsen seemed as surprised and puzzled by the remark as I was. Kenny only looked vaguely annoyed.

"What about lawyers," I asked. I had forgotten completely about Mrs. Baker's previous plans to change her will.

Ingrid tossed her head in a haughty manner that meant she disapproved of my tone. "Kenny's back, isn't he?" she said.

I understood then what she was talking about. With Kenny back, and reconciled with his mother, it was likely that she would leave the farm to him, and not will it to the church, as she had previously mentioned she might do.

Apparently Ingrid had discussed the subject, and the possible change in the will, with Kenny, because it was plain from his expression that he too knew what she was talking about.

I was suddenly angry with her for bringing the subject up, and angrier still to realize that it was a subject that she and Kenny had discussed between them. He had been home for only a short time, and in that time he should have been concerned with just being here and reacquainting himself with the farm and its inhabitants, particularly his mother. Yet already he was thinking ahead, thinking to his inheritance. And if I could judge from Ingrid's remark, he fully expected that it would be his.

Probably he had a right to think of such things. As a man who had always considered himself practical, I could not honestly say that, in his position, I wouldn't do the same thing. Even with her display of new strength, Mrs. Baker still stood on the brink. The faintest wind might upset the balance and send her into the darkness beyond. If Kenny expected to be her heir, and wanted to inherit this place, he would have to consider these questions now, before fate and the ill health of an old woman answered them for him.

It was a practical matter, to be considered calmly and logically—but it was not a very pleasant one. And to my way of thinking, it did not speak very well for the dark young man seated across from me, looking annoyed with Ingrid for having broached the subject at all.

I stood abruptly. "I think," I said to Ingrid, "That you would do better to stick to things that concern you."

Ingrid had long ago outgrown letting me have the last word on any matter. "And I think you should stop deciding what does and does not concern me," she said.

I let it go at that and started angrily from the room. As I passed Olsen, I saw her look from Kenny to Ingrid, and she wore a puzzled expression. I wondered what the question was that she was turning over in her mind.

KENNY'S BACK, BY VICTOR J. BANIS

CHAPTER SEVEN

The days that followed were not unpleasant ones. For me it was a busy period: finishing up the summer work and seeing to the fall planting. Our warm weather had run out abruptly, just as Olsen had predicted, and the days were growing rapidly cooler.

"It's going to be an early winter," Olsen informed me, ignoring weather predictions to the contrary. "And a long, hard one. I think we'll do some extra canning. You'd better try to get the outside work done early, too."

I think the fall of the year was my favorite time. That may have been in part the result of working with the land and the crops, and seeing the results of that labor. It was a time when everything seemed multiplied and bountiful. There were wonderful things to see and smell. To my mind, nothing has ever matched the aroma of fresh hay, or the sight of baskets of produce stacked outside the kitchen, waiting to be put up for the winter.

Olsen worked with the neighbor women as she did each fall. She would go to their places and help put up their output of fruit and vegetables, bringing home her share for her work. Then, they would appear in turn at the pink house, fifteen or twenty women canning fresh tomatoes or peaches or tart red cherries in and around the big kitchen. The scents of food and the happy working chatter of the women carried out even past the barn.

Everywhere, too, was the golden autumn air, crisp and clear, so buoyant that you seemed almost to be walking above the ground rather than on it.

I followed Olsen's advice and worked hard to get the outside work finished as quickly as possible, before a sudden winter caught us unprepared. As a result, I saw less of Kenny than might otherwise have been the case. When I did see him, one of us was coming or going, and the meetings were only in brief passing.

I'd thought that perhaps he would begin to take an interest in the farm again, and for a few days I kept expecting him to show up where we were working. For the present, however, he apparently had other things on his mind. Some of them I didn't want to think about. One of the most obvious, though, was Ingrid.

They had taken to one another at once, in a way quite unlike their relationship of the past. Ingrid seemed to have taken possession of Kenny's time and energies, and if he minded he kept his objections to himself. They were always together, in and around the house.

This was something that I had not considered when we had first learned that Kenny was coming back, although the possibility should have been obvious. Kenny had grown into a man, and a very handsome one who had added maturity to that inescapable charm he had always possessed. Ingrid was an attractive young woman who, I judged, had already had one experience with romance and was apparently ripe for another. It was probably inevitable that they should have captured one another's interest.

In all fairness to Kenny, a great deal of his interest and attention, not to mention time, were devoted to his mother. He spent as much of his time with her as was possible, or at least practical. If she was up during the day he was in the house or on the porch with her. If there was even a possibility that she might be up, he stayed near so that he could join her if she decided she had the strength to stir from her room. Only on those days when Olsen declared it "highly unlikely" that Mrs. Baker would be out of bed, did Kenny go far from the house.

At first I regarded this as the logical excuse for his not coming out into the fields. But the fact was, when he was free and could get away from the house, he did not use the opportunity to come looking after the work—or me. He and Ingrid had things of their own to do. I heard about some of them, others I didn't.

If I say that Kenny showed no interest in the business of the farm, I mean that he showed no interest directly to me, and that he had no inclination to take part in any of the work of running the farm. For whatever reason, however, he was not entirely without some interest in the place, as became apparent during the next week or so.

I might have been pleased with this, except that Kenny's concern for farming matters was quite a different thing from what it had been in the past, judging from the indications. In the past, he had loved it for itself. He had loved the earth and working it, and seeing it bring forth life of myriad sorts. As to the business end of it, he had cared not in the slightest for that.

Somewhere, in the time he had been gone, he had acquired a taste for business matters. If he talked about the farm now, it was in terms of what it produced, the prices each crop would bring, plans for the following season, and such things that hadn't interested him before.

"How much will you make off the hay this year?" he asked one evening, while Olsen and I were discussing the season just ending.

Surprised, but at the same time a little flattered by his interest, I told him about what we would make.

"Same as last year, isn't it?" he said. He was thinking aloud more than commenting to me, but the comment struck a raw nerve in me.

"Is it?" I asked quickly, looking in Ingrid's direction. I knew well enough that he was right. If I had been so inclined, I could have given him the total figures for the last three or four years, but I had never made a policy of discussing those figures with anyone but Olsen or Mrs. Baker herself. Apparently someone had no such scruples.

Either he saw the look I gave Ingrid, or he read my thoughts. "My mother went over some of the books with me," he explained, directing his attention to me again.

I felt a slight embarrassment over my suspicions but they were not without some foundation. All of a sudden, Ingrid too had acquired considerable interest in the farm, particularly in the business aspects of it. This, in a girl who had rarely thought beyond which color was best for her or whether her hair was too long or too short, was a surprising development—and, when one gave it some thought, not a very pleasant one.

It was Ingrid who had first pointed out one particular significance of Kenny's return: the effect it might have for her, Olsen, and myself. When we had come to the place, Kenny had been a kid and Mrs. Baker a window who even then was in poor health. She had needed someone to take over running things for her, at least until Kenny was old enough to run it himself.

When Kenny left, of course we had become even more firmly entrenched. With Mrs. Baker more and more confined to her room, and eventually to her bed, we had to run the farm almost as though we in fact were its owners, and by and large, we lived well for people who were really nothing more than hired help.

But Kenny was back now, and in the way of once again becoming heir to the land. When he did, it was obvious that we would become mere farmhands again. It was even possible that he would have no great need of our services. Certainly a young man in the prime of his life and health wouldn't need a manager for a farm that he could as easily manage himself.

For the most part, I can't say that these prospects particularly worried me. At the very least, I was sure that Kenny would keep on Olsen, should he become the owner of the Baker farm. He would need a housekeeper, and I knew that he felt almost a son's affection for Olsen.

As for myself, I was hardly a doddering old man. It was unlikely that I would want for a job, even if Kenny found he had no need for me. I'd had more than a few offers over the years, from farmers who had found something to admire in the way I ran this place. Had it not been for my personal feelings, and ties to the place and the Bakers, I might even have bettered myself by changing jobs. But I had my reasons for staying where I was—so long as I was wanted or needed.

For Ingrid, however, it was a different story, although this was the first I had really given any thought to the matter. For one thing, there was her pride. I couldn't imagine that she would take very well to becoming a hired hand again, with the possibility that she might even have to do some work to retain that status. Ingrid was far more decorative than useful.

She had few other possibilities, unfortunately. We were hardly rich enough that she could retire into leisure. Without a doubt, she could marry, and though she had remained aloof from most people, she had received her share of proposals. Ingrid was not likely to marry just any young and willing man from Hanover, however. The likelihood that she would become an ordinary farm wife with the attendant hard work and lack of fun and frivolity was a very slim one. I could more likely imagine Ingrid married to some up-and-coming businessman. At the very least, she might settle for a particularly well-off farmer, someone with enough of an income to hire a housekeeper to do the work, and who could afford lots of pretty dresses and trinkets for her. If her farmer were someone young and attractive, someone she knew well and could even be genuinely affectionate with, maybe even love, so much the better.

I would never say that Ingrid's interest in Kenny was purely a business one. God knows, she had every reason to be physically attracted to him. Most everyone else was, it seemed. And they had almost grown up together, which must have produced some sincere feelings of affection between them.

Nevertheless, I wasn't fool enough to believe that it was love alone that inspired Ingrid's sudden new interest in matters pertaining to the management and the income of the Baker farm. The more obvious her interest became, the more I suspected and disliked her motives.

I fought against my suspicions, and most especially against the resentment that accompanied them. I didn't admire myself for being jealous and for concerning myself with things were really none of my business. If she had set her sights on Kenny, regardless of her motives, that was her business and Kenny's, not mind. He was no fool, surely. If he realized her intentions, and had no objections to them, who was I to complain?

There were times, though, that despite my best efforts my feelings on this matter did become obvious. These were the times when Ingrid overstepped the boundaries of what I considered to be my territory, the running of the farm. In time, the farm might be Kenny's, might eventually even be Ingrid's, but for the present I was still managing it for Mrs. Baker and I had never cared much for any interference on that score.

There were several occasions when the feelings on this subject came into the open, briefly, but not very pleasantly. One of them came up because of a slight setback in Mrs. Baker's condition. It was apparently no more serious than several others she'd had, but it meant that for a day or two she was confined to her bed and saw no one except Olsen. As a result, Kenny had a day or two of freedom. As had become customary, he spent this time with Ingrid.

I came down one morning to a surprise that at first was amusing: the information that Ingrid was already up, and out of the house

"I never thought she'd be up this early unless the house was on fire," I commented in answer to Olsen's information. My amusement didn't last very long, however.

"They took the Jeep, she and Kenny," Olsen added.

"Well, of all the damn nonsense!" I sputtered, almost choking on a mouthful of coffee. "Didn't you tell them I had to use it today?"

"I mentioned it," she said, setting my breakfast on the table rather loudly. The set of her chin told me she agreed with my evaluation of the matter, and disapproved also; but at the same time, Olsen was not one to criticize much of what Kenny did, and she was stubbornly set on not doing so now either. "You could take the Buick."

"So could they. Where did they go, anyway?"

"For a ride." The bread landed on the table hard enough to splash my coffee over the rim of the cup. Olsen knew where it was they had gone. She also was going to keep that information to herself.

My curiosity was in high gear by this time, but I knew better than to try to question her on the subject—and I'd have cut my tongue off before asking Kenny and Ingrid when they came back, which wasn't until evening. Fortunately, I didn't have to. Ingrid gave me the answer herself, over the supper table.

"We were at the gray house," she said out of the clear, making a very casual remark out of it, but Olsen had a wary air about her, as though she expected problems, and Kenny was unusually silent. Apparently this was Ingrid's turn at bat.

The gray house was the one on the other farm, the small one that had been rented before and was now empty. It was about forty miles away, a rough drive in the old Jeep. The fact that they had taken the Jeep instead of the comfortable Buick sedan meant that they had also looked the place over pretty thoroughly. They'd have needed the Jeep to get back into the fields and the places the Buick couldn't safely go.

I said nothing, concentrating my attention on my food and waiting for Ingrid to get to the point. She was leading up to something, and I had a pretty good idea what, but I wasn't rushing her—or making it any easier for her, either.

"It's a shame it's not being worked," Ingrid went on finally when it became apparent I wasn't going to offer any comment just yet. "Everyone says it's good land. It used to produce pretty well when it was worked, didn't it?"

"Fair," I said, helping myself to another slice of beef.

"Oughtn't it to be worked?" She was not going to be put off by roast beef.

"Well, now that you mention it," I said, leaning back a little in my chair and looking square at her for the first time, "That might not be a bad idea. Why don't you take it over, Ingrid? You could work that land and that would leave us free to run this place without any interference."

Her face reddened, but she refused to be sidetracked into a quarrel about her laziness. She had another quarrel in mind.

"We could rent it out again," she said. "The Halvorsens did well with it. And Kenny thought that if the trees were cleared out of the west end...."

"I don't think *we* should be worrying about it," I interrupted her. I had heard all I wanted to hear. "If Mrs. Baker doesn't see any need to rent it out, that's her business. And if I don't see fit to recommend it, that's my business.

Her face went full crimson this time, but she wasn't about to give up yet. "Kenny agrees with me," she said, her voice rising. "And it's his business more than anyone else's."

"Is it?" I asked. I was trying hard not to sound as mad as I felt. "The last I heard, I was still running this farm for its owner. Or maybe we have a new owner and someone forgot to mention it to me." I said the last to Kenny, turning to face him.

"Mar," Olsen said, trying to fend off the brewing clash. "Hadn't you better remember Kenny's place here?"

She successfully stopped the rest that I was going to say—and she was right, of course, I had no business speaking as I had to Kenny.

Kenny knew a losing fight, though, and maybe he felt a war could better be won by losing a battle. Either that, or the blow that I had landed below the belt had taken the fight out of him.

"Mar's right," he said quietly. "He runs this farm for my mother, and offhand I'd say he runs it well. Anyway, it's for her to decide whether he does or he doesn't."

Ingrid wasn't a good loser. She looked just then as though she could have taken us both on, and for once the looks she gave Kenny weren't very adoring.

"I think we've had enough bickering for one supper," Olsen said with a note of finality.

"I've had more than enough," Ingrid said sharply, standing with a quick movement and flinging her napkin across her plate, "Of quite a few things." Having fired that shot, she retreated in a flurry of swishing skirts and tossing hair.

70

"I'm sorry," I said to the room in general, and I genuinely was. "I guess I lost my temper."

"I'd forgotten you had one," Kenny said with an easy laugh.

I didn't answer him. I was thinking that if someone tried to keep a list of the things Kenny had forgotten since he'd been gone, it would take a hell of a long sheet of paper.

KENNY'S BACK, BY VICTOR J. BANIS

CHAPTER EIGHT

Black Creek runs for a good mile or so across Baker property before it reaches Hanover and divides the town in two. I've been told that the name had to do with one of the town's original settlers rather than the color of the waterway in question, but there are places along Black Creek where the name seems appropriate enough. In spots it runs deep and wide, and where the trees hang far out over its surface, hiding it from the sun, the water appears dark and bottomless. Some of these serve as swimming holes for the young men about the town, One in particular had been "our" hole, Kenny's and mine, and far enough from town that nobody else ever went there.

I knew from experience that those swimming holes, including ours, are not as bottomless as they look, however. Beneath the covering darkness of the surface water, there are rocks and fallen tree limbs about which the fast water swirls and rushes, creating dangerous undercurrents in contradiction to the smooth surface.

Further along, though, the creek runs shallow. Without the depth, the water looks clear, and the rocks and debris extend above the surface or are plainly visible beneath it. Here the many currents and the water's swift, uneven progress are obvious. It foams and splashes, swirls threateningly around a boulder, changes directions, and rushes on dangerously, providing a challenge to more than one young man who's tried, sometimes unsuccessfully, to ride these "little rapids."

It was like that at the farm. With Kenny's return, and reconciliation with his parent, things seemed at first to be smooth and tranquil. The dangers and the difficulties that existed were like so many hidden obstructions. Concealed beneath the dark surface, they could only be sensed or guessed at. I thought I knew of them, and in that respect considered myself more knowledgeable than the others. But while some of them—Dexter, Ingrid's scheming, Kenny's desire to gain ownership of the property—were known to me, there were others whose presence I had not yet come to suspect.

With the quarrel between Ingrid and me, however, the waters began to run shallow, and gradually many matters that had been hidden began to near the surface.

Of course, it was not an all-at-once thing. Rather, the stream of events ran less smoothly now. Here they veered, there they rippled unevenly, signs of what lay ahead. If I had been brighter, I might have read them for what they were, but though I have never thought of myself as stupid, I lacked the quick grasp of things that some men have. I reasoned slowly, and learned more through stubborn persistence than through my intellectual instinct. I was aware that something was coming up, and that there were matters that lay hidden beneath the surface, but I was not yet able to identify them.

This was far from the first time Ingrid and I had quarreled. There was hardly a week in our lives that we hadn't found something to disagree about, and Olsen said time and again that she had never known two blood relatives who could bicker so much or be as often at one another's throats. It was inevitable, I suppose, considering our natures, which were so vastly different.

I was born to a relatively simple life, I think, and I set more store on comfort than on excitement. I disliked change and even as a youngster had been pretty set in my ways. If I was slow to reach a decision, I was slower yet to change my mind on any point, and stubborn enough to cling to my own way of thinking, even in the face of evidence that I was wrong. If my few virtues were ever weighed in the balance against my generous supply of faults, it wasn't hard to see which way the scales would go, and if I was ever to pass the sort of final judgment Olsen liked to warn me about, it would only be through the efforts of a sharp lawyer.

Ingrid shared my stubbornness, but that and blonde hair were about the only things we had in common. She was quick and bright, and she saw things with a purposefulness that was usually blind to any considerations but her own. There was no single element of her personality that wasn't mirrored by an equal and opposite aspect, as though two separate and distinct people shared her small body. If she was kind one day, she could be equally cruel the next. For every generous act, she had a selfish one. Every question that presented itself to her was worthy, it seemed, of at least two opinions, and she could leap from one to the other without any hesitation and seemly with no realization that she had changed directions. But if she was adept at changing courses, she was equally firm in resisting any attempts by anyone else to deter her from whatever goal she pursued, and only her own inconstancy prevented her from achieving her every ambition.

In the past, Ingrid had been as quick to make up as she was to pick a fight, and she had more often that not set herself to coaxing me out of my sulks with the same resoluteness she had shown in angering me. This time, however, it was different. Whatever her schemes were, Ingrid had determined to see them through, and she was not likely to tolerate interference from any quarter, least of all from me.

From the evening of our quarrel over the un-rented property, Ingrid remained cool toward me and aloof. I'd have been worse than a fool if I'd suspected for a moment that she had given up any of her ideas, regarding either Kenny or the farm. She had made up her mind that the income of the properties could be increased, and on that point she was undeniably correct.

The difference was that from my standpoint, and from what I assumed Mrs. Baker's to be, there was no reason why they should be. From Ingrid's standpoint, however, increased income was reason enough in itself, particularly if, as became increasingly likely, she might someday share in that bounty.

So she continued her investigation of the farm's operations, and whatever lack of farming knowledge she had, she made up for with a keen intelligence and an eye for potential profit. The only difference in her tactics was that she did not quite go for a direct confrontation with me, but went about her efforts as though they concerned me not at all.

It was an uneven match from the beginning. For the moment, I was the manager of the property, but that was the only thing in my favor. Ingrid had a specific goal, which gave additional impetus to her effort, and she was certainly sharper and cleverer than I. More to the point, she was quick to enlist the aid of allies whose influence on me and on Mrs. Baker was certain to have more effect than her own arguments. It was obvious that Kenny shared her point of view, though he was not as keen as she was to argue it. And I needed no second sight to see that Ingrid was taking her case to the high court: Mrs. Baker herself.

The setback that Mrs. Baker had suffered, while not disastrous, had been sufficient to throw a bit of a scare into all of us, herself included. As a result, she gave in to Olsen's firm demands and appeared less often out of her room.

For whatever motives, Kenny played the role of a good son, and as his mother could not now come out to see him, he went regularly to see her. He spent a part of each day visiting with her in her rooms.

For the most part there was nothing mysterious about these visits. Sometimes the doors were open, and sometimes closed, but even when the doors were closed, Olsen was in and out numerous times, on legitimate errands or often merely to assure herself that her patient was not being unduly excited in any way.

From Olsen I had a pretty good picture of what went on. Kenny and his mother talked or, occasionally, he would be coaxed into reading to her, although he had never been enthusiastic about reading. Having heard his reading voice, I couldn't imagine that it was a very entertaining time for any of them, but Mrs. Baker seemed to enjoy it well enough.

It was apparent, however, that these daily visits were not without Ingrid's influence, nor did she try to conceal that fact from me. It was no secret that she frequently went with Kenny to his mother's rooms. The only explanation that was offered came from Kenny, who was glad to have someone with him to take over the chore of reading aloud. I was fully aware, of course, that there was more than charity behind my sister's sudden interest in a woman whom she had scarcely seen or talked to in the last year. I wondered how much of this was apparent to Mrs. Baker, who had retained a pretty keen intelligence despite her failing health.

For Kenny's part, I had begun to see that he was not above some scheming of his own, besides sharing in Ingrid's plans. At first, I wondered about his willingness to go along with Ingrid when her motives must have been obvious to him also, but, as matters advanced, I had gradually come to suspect that his motives might not be much different from hers.

Despite the fact that Kenny had been to all appearances forgiven, and had been home for a moment almost, there was still nothing definite about the will, whether it would be changed or not. So far as any of us could say, Mrs. Baker still intended to leave the estate to the church.

Obviously, Kenny wanted the farm, and if Ingrid expected to profit from her growing friendship with Kenny, she wanted him to have it also. Only one person could accomplish that goal for them: Mrs. Baker.

There was one possible explanation for the fact that the bedridden widow had allowed this question to remain up in the air. It occurred to me finally, and it must have occurred to Kenny much sooner, considering his greater interest in the question.

Kenny had created a full-scale scandal by being discovered in a homosexual relationship. He was now at an age when most of the young men born and raised around Hanover were already husbands and fathers. Kenny was not. It might have been that Mrs. Baker still had some doubts, and perhaps she too had thought of Dexter Holloman, and wondered if that entire affair might not be repeated now that Kenny was back.

If such were the case, Kenny's task would be to convince her otherwise, in order to complete his reconciliation. What better way to do this than to convince her that his interests, in fact, lay elsewhere, and that perhaps he was even on his way to joining the ranks of young, married Hanover men?

I tried to tell myself that I was being unfair. It was entirely possible that the increasing signs of affection between Kenny and Ingrid were entirely genuine. No doubt Kenny must have felt some fondness for Ingrid in the past. That fact that he had written to her when he decided to return indicated that fondness was more than I had suspected. Still, I couldn't help being dubious of this blossoming romance, nor could I help the fact that Kenny seemed to me less admirable for it.

Ingrid did not limit her efforts entirely to Mrs. Baker and Kenny, either. Olsen, too, had come under her influence, which was not so surprising in view of the fact that Ingrid had always managed her mother rather well. I was surprised, however, that Olsen had been swayed so quickly, and that she went so far as to press the point with me, something she did rarely.

"Seems a shame we don't do more winter planting," she commented in an overly nonchalant manner one evening, when just the two of us were in the kitchen. "It wouldn't take a great deal of work for what we'd get out of it."

I answered her as quickly, and as sharply, as I had answered Ingrid. "I don't think there's any need for it," I told her, rising angrily from the table. "But maybe you ought to mention it to Mrs. Baker. She may have changed her mind about it by now."

We were both immediately sorry, of course, Olsen for having interfered in my work, and I for having snapped back at her, but the apologies remained unsaid, and I suspected that Olsen thought I was at least partially wrong.

I thought about it later, in my room that night, and I even began to wonder if maybe I was wrong, and everyone else right. I was holding out stubbornly on a point that was undoubtedly going to be changed. Sooner or later, Kenny and Ingrid between them were certain to persuade Mrs.

78

Baker to their way of thinking, and I would end up doing exactly what they wanted, increasing the farm's output and its income. What was I holding out for, then? I didn't know, yet at the same time I continued to hold fast to my opinion, and Ingrid continued just as stubbornly to advance hers.

If I had been brighter, no doubt I could have found a motive for my stubbornness. It was there, and things began to happen which should have made it all plain to me, but I was too slow to understand them, and by the time I had grasped their significance, I was too late to prevent what happened.

That was a fact for which I was to have considerable regrets—but that was not until the stream had reached the rapids, and we had all been caught up inescapably in its swift, dangerous current.

KENNY'S BACK, BY VICTOR J. BANIS

CHAPTER NINE

Without knowing just what, I expected something to happen. I didn't expect it to come the way it did, though, or from the quarter that it did. Of all the inhabitants of the Baker farm who might have changed the course of events, Jezebel was surely the least likely.

Since the occasion behind the barn, when the mare had nipped his hand, Kenny had not done any riding, nor even been around the horses except coincidentally. I wondered about this, but without attaching any particular importance to it. If Kenny had decided that he no longer cared for animals, or for riding horses, that was his privilege. He wasn't the first man to have lost his taste for them, or the knack. His explanation that he hadn't been around a horse since he had left was reasonable enough, and if he had let it go at that, chances are I'd never have suspected otherwise.

If it had been up to Kenny alone, he probably would have let it go at that. Obviously he had no desire to try his hand at something as well left alone. Jezebel had gotten old and didn't have too much riding left in her, and probably no great enthusiasm for that. With luck, Kenny might never have been put to a test.

Ingrid, however, was not one to wait patiently if there was an opportunity to move boldly forward. This was a matter that concerned her also, as I was eventually to learn, and she got her way in this as she did in most matters. She convinced Kenny that he would have to ride, for reasons that only the two of them could then understand—and he tried.

They chose a day when by rights they should have had the place to themselves. I was out in the field, checking on the last of the fence repairs. Olsen had gone into town on her weekly errands, and this time, Pete had ridden in with her to take care of some matters of his own. Except for Mrs. Baker, asleep in her room, Kenny and Ingrid were alone around the house.

Rather, they should have been, but for once luck wasn't with them. The Jeep, which I was driving, picked this particular morning to display a little of its own temper, and went out on me before I even reached the fence.

I knew what the trouble was: I had been intending for a week to replace a faulty distributor cap. The knowledge that I was at fault, however, didn't do much to improve my mood, nor did the realization that the new part was back in the barn and that, before I could get the Jeep running again, I'd have to hike back to the barn and get it. With an occasional "Damn it to hell," under my breath, I started back, walking fast.

The place was quiet when I got there, and I wondered vaguely if Kenny and Ingrid were off on another wild-goose chase, but I didn't attach too much importance to that thought. I had other things on my mind at the time.

I went straight to the barn, which was open. Pete had set up a tool room and a makeshift workshop to one side of the barn as one came in, and the distributor cap was there, just where I had left it. I got it and was on my way out when Ladyship, whose stall was at the end, whinnied. When I looked in her direction, I saw that the other stall, where Jezebel should have been, was open and empty.

There had been rumors about some prowlers in the area and some thefts. My first thought was that someone had seen the place apparently deserted and the barn open, and had taken the mare, although if I had thought about that a little longer, I'd have realized that Jezebel was not the mostly likely thing for a burglar to steal. I started for her stall to investigate, but as I approached it, I heard voices from out back, and I followed them instead.

82

I recognized Ingrid's voice first, maybe because she was speaking more urgently. "You've got to," she said in a firm voice.

"I don't know if I can." That was Kenny's voice. By this time, I had reached the door that led out into the pen in which the horses were exercised. I don't know what it was that made me pause. I wasn't in the habit of eavesdropping, and I hadn't consciously intended to do so this time, but something made me stop inside the barn, out of sight, for a moment.

"Try," Ingrid said. "She's gotten old. She'll be safe."

It was a moment more before I understood Kenny's lack of reply. I had been waiting to hear his answer without realizing that Ingrid had won her argument. Not until I heard Jezebel's complaining snort did I realize that Kenny had mounted her. When I did, I moved at once.

Jezebel was old, Ingrid was right about that, but she was every bit as unpredictable and temperamental as she had ever been. Even before, when Kenny had been more at home in a saddle, I had never felt safe about his riding Jezebel, and she was by no means a horse to be ridden by a man who had lost the feel for them, and especially one who was apparently afraid. Horses sense that.

"Kenny!" I yelled as I came through the door into the pen, and then I stopped. Kenny had ridden her out to the center of the pen. He looked a little uncertain but he sat well in the saddle, and he had the appearance of a man who knew horses. If I had looked first, I might not have yelled. I might have given him a chance to try his skill.

But I hadn't waited, I had yelled first, and my alarmed voice set off a chain reaction. I hadn't counted on how much my sudden appearance and my shout would startle all three of them, thinking themselves alone as they did. Kenny jerked around in his saddle, forgetting completely that he was on a horse and not in an easy chair. My yell, Ingrid's startled squeal and Kenny's sudden move were more than Jezebel was likely to take without reaction. She snorted, kicked and reared with a suddenness that would have done well at unseating a good rider who was paying attention to what he was doing. Kenny wasn't either, and he went sailing.

In her young days, Jezebel would have given him hell at this point, but I think if the truth were known, she was probably the most surprised of all. It had been years since she'd even had a rider on her, and she must have forgotten what it was like to give one the toss. She jumped and shook herself, as though determining that he was really gone from her back, and then she spun around to stare at the fallen rider, as if wondering what he had planned next.

For a moment, Ingrid and I were both frozen. Kenny had fallen hard and he lay motionless on the ground, out cold, or maybe worse.

Ingrid screamed again, breaking the spell that had held us rooted to the spot. "Kenny?" she cried. She was outside the pen and she started now to scramble over the fence.

"Stay out of there," I yelled, yanking her back to the ground. I cleared the fence in what seemed like one leap and started to run toward Kenny. Jezebel was still beside him, and at the sight of my presence in the pen, she reared again, not so much threatening as frightened by all the commotion.

Scared as I was for Kenny, I had the horse to think of first. She looked more like a scared kid than a dangerous animal, but I knew enough to realize that fear could be more dangerous in an animal than temper. Her hooves were cutting the air, and without meaning to do us harm, she could have sent Kenny and me both on our way to the next world.

"Easy, girl, easy," I spoke to her in a coaxing voice. I caught the rein on my second grab, trying hard to stay out of the way of those hooves, and at the same time keep myself between her and Kenny's body.

She quieted easily. Probably she was glad to have someone in charge. She snorted again and her nostrils flared with her excited breathing, but she stayed down and leaned against my hand when I petted her neck. Still talking to her in low, calm tones, I led her as quickly as I could back into the barn. Ingrid waited until we were out of the pen before she climbed the fence and ran to Kenny;.

"He's out cold," she said, unnecessarily, as I came back out. Her eyes were huge with fear, and her face had gone stark white.

"He's lucky he didn't break his damn neck," I said, none too politely. I was scared too, of course, and I usually showed fear by getting angry.

He hadn't broken his neck, at least. It was hard to tell how much damage had been done, though. I gathered the limp body up in my arms and started for the house. Ingrid ran ahead, opening gates and doors for me. We didn't talk. If we had, I'd probably have torn into her like a cyclone. It had been a crazy, stupid thing to do, and the fact that Kenny wasn't dead was due more to chance than anything else.

Kenny was no featherweight. In my excitement I had picked him up and carried him without difficulty, but I was glad when we reached his room and I could lay him across his bed. I started unbuttoning his jacket at once.

"I'll have to take his clothes off," I said without looking up.

"I'm not a child, Mar. I'm used to...."

I wasn't interested in hearing whatever it was that Ingrid was used to now that she was no longer a child. Fortunately, I didn't have to say so. She understood the look I gave her, and she had enough sense to know better than to argue the point just now.

"I'll wait outside," she finished lamely.

"Go call a doctor," I said.

She hesitated at that. Whatever she had on her mind, it must have been pretty serious for her to risk disagreeing with me, knowing the mood I was in just at that moment

"Do we have to?" she asked meekly.

"Christ, Ingrid, he's just been thrown from a horse. For all we know...."

"Couldn't you tell if there are, well, any bones broken?"

I looked up and swallowed the words I was going to shout at her. She was scared, more scared even than she had been by the fall. I didn't know what it was all about, but I knew that Ingrid was pleading desperately with me.

"I'll take a look," I said begrudgingly. "Wait downstairs."

She went without further argument, relieved to have gained even a partial concession from me. I wasn't sure just what it was I had conceded, but at the moment I had other things on my mind.

If I had stopped to think of what I was doing, I might never have been able to go through with it. I had spent years dreaming of Kenny's body. In my mind, I had remembered every inch of it, naked and beautiful. I had desired it with an ache that had left me trembling and sick.

Now, unexpectedly, I was removing his clothing, stripping him bare until the body that I remembered was exposed before me. I ran my hands over the firm flesh, probing, groping, searching for some sign of serious injury—and, astonishingly, during the entire time, the other thoughts, the memory of what the naked body on the bed had once meant to me, never crossed my mind.

Aside from a rapidly swelling lump on his head and a good number of bruises, the worst damage I found was a long splinter that had been driven an inch, maybe two, into his arm.

"Okay, Doctor," I told myself, probing the spot gently, "We may as well operate on that."

I took a penknife from my pocket and looked around for a match to sterilize it with. There weren't any in sight, and without much thinking about what I was doing, I pulled open the drawer of Kenny's dresser.

At first I didn't notice the papers there. I pushed them aside and found a book of matches beneath them. In doing so, however, I had uncovered one single sheet, crumpled as though at some time it had been crushed into a wad and afterward been smoothed out again.

There was nothing on it but Kenny's name—but the name had been written over and over again, in every available inch of space. Without thinking, I picked it up and stared at it.

Why would a man fill a sheet of paper with his own signature, I wondered—and especially when, if you looked closely, the writing didn't all seem quite as though it matched? Some of the signatures were written large, some of them small, some of them leaned far over to the right, and others stood straighter. It looked as though the writer had been trying to disguise his handwriting—or change it.

I realized suddenly that this was something personal, from Kenny's drawer, something I had no business even seeing. Blushing, although I had been unobserved, I returned the paper to the dresser. As I did so, my eyes went automatically to the other papers.

They were mostly letters, from what I could see of them. I had no intention of looking at them, or examining them, but even the one glance was sufficient to tell me one thing: at least one of them, the top envelope, was in Ingrid's handwriting.

In itself that shouldn't have been too surprising. I already knew that she had written to Kenny, to let him know that it was all right for him to come home. At the time, he had been in Indiana, and this envelope was addressed to Indianapolis. I looked at it long enough to see that. The puzzling part, though, was that it was not addressed to Kenny, but to someone named Douglas Allen.

I closed the drawer with a quick, impulsive movement, but the image of the envelope stayed before my eyes. The name was unfamiliar to me. Ingrid's mysterious boyfriend, I wondered? That was possible, but it left unanswered another question. How had the letter—or letters, since there had been a stack of them, although I didn't know that they were all necessarily addressed the same—how had it come to be in Kenny's possession?

I turned back to the unconscious man on the bed, and for the first time I saw him not as someone who had been hurt and whom I was examining, but as a naked young man. I realized then why the sight of his nudity had not aroused me the way even the memory of it had always done. It was not the same body that had haunted my dreams for these past five years.

It looked the same, of course, in many ways—but Kenny had changed and, seeing him like this, the changes were more obvious than they had been before, perhaps because this was the way I most often remembered him.

He was still handsome. He looked now as though he were sleeping, but even in repose I could see lines and flaws that I hadn't remembered. I noticed a faint scar below one ear that hadn't been there before. Some fight he'd been in during those five years? His dark hair still spilled across his forehead, but in the past, the sun had painted highlights into it that were missing now. Apparently Kenny had not been in the sun as much during his absence. That would explain, too, the fact that he was paler.

My eyes moved slowly down the length of his body—longer and leaner than I remembered it. There was a white outline of a bathing suit. That hadn't been there before, but of course, as often as we had been swimming together, there had never been a bathing suit to leave a mark. Wherever it was he had been, they didn't go bare-ass swimming. I almost grinned as I imagined how uncomfortable Kenny must have been with that restriction.

He'd grown in other ways, too. *He finally made it,* I thought, staring at the cock that stretched limply over one thigh. The little son of a bitch was bigger now than I was, just as he'd always predicted. For a moment, I was even amused.

So Kenny hadn't stopped growing, at eighteen. Some guys didn't. I knew that. Five years of growing and changing, years in which there hadn't been as much sun, and no naked swimming, and no horses. Time to forget things, little things—like how to write his name. Time to meet someone named Douglas Allen, in Indianapolis, who got letters from Ingrid, and later gave them to Kenny.

I suddenly realized I was shaking. I bent down and lifted the bedspread up over the bed, covering Kenny's torso with it. Then, working fast, I put the match to the knife blade and cut the splinter out of his arm. It was a nasty looking thing but it had not gone deep, and removing it was a minor operation. I put my handkerchief over the slight bleeding and went to the bathroom for iodine. Kenny stirred slightly and groaned when I put the burning liquid on the cut. I worked even faster putting a bandage over it. Somehow I didn't want to be here with him when he woke up. I wanted to be away from him. I wanted to think, to try to remember…and I couldn't think clearly with him before me like this.

He kicked off the bedspread before I left. I stared hard at him for a long moment, feeling a dryness in my throat. Then, remembering that Ingrid would want to see him, and Olsen, too, I pulled the covers back and got him under them, despite hands that were shaking.

Ingrid was just coming up the stairs when I came out into the hall. "He's okay, I think," I told her. "There's a nasty bump on his head. You'd maybe better put a cold cloth on that."

She was relieved, of course, but there was something more in her face, too. I must have looked shaken. She gave me a puzzled look and I think she wanted to say something, but I was in no mood for conversation just then. I went by her without waiting for her comments. As I reached my own room, I heard her going into Kenny's.

It wasn't much easier trying to think in my own room. I smoked a cigarette and stared from the window. I reminded myself I should be in the fields. It was almost noon and so far I hadn't gotten any work done. The Jeep was still waiting for its distributor cap that I had dropped somewhere in the barn.

I could see him, I could hear him, yelling and laughing in that total way of his—but the memories were blurred suddenly. They kept receding from me when I most wanted them clear.

I opened a drawer of my own dresser and from far back in a corner I removed the single picture I had kept of him. It was only a snapshot, one of those group things where everyone looks stiff and unnatural—everyone except Kenny. He stood with his languid grace, his head to one side, a cocky grin on his face. I studied the picture and then I moved to the window and studied it again in the light.

It was hard to tell. I couldn't be sure.

I'd wondered since his return about the changes in Kenny. So many of them—and there were perfectly reasonable explanations for them all, of course. But there was another explanation that had suddenly occurred to me, one that wasn't at all reasonable.

It was crazy, impossible to believe, and yet it was there, buzzing around in my head, repeating itself over and over. Kenny has changed, Kenny has changed—or else—or else, Kenny wasn't Kenny at all.

KENNY'S BACK, BY VICTOR J. BANIS

CHAPTER TEN

As it turned out, my diagnosis of Kenny's condition was pretty much accurate. There was no apparent damage beyond a nasty bump on his head, a few bruises, and some stiff limbs that made themselves obvious in his movements for a few days. At least, that was all the physical damage. It was quite clear, though, that his pride had suffered considerably. He was embarrassed when he saw me again, and even shamefaced around the others, who of course had learned about the accident.

I think that Ingrid had halfway hoped that the accident might be kept a secret from the rest of the household. Looking back on it, this may have been what she wanted to say to me in the hall when I left Kenny's room, but my manner hadn't been very encouraging, and apparently they had decided to ride out the embarrassment—and whatever suspicions the accident might have raised, if that thought occurred to them.

The suspicions were mine alone, so far as I knew. And even in my mind they were still too unformed and too vague to take seriously. It was only a possibility that had occurred to me and that, as yet, seemed too incredible to put any credence in. At the same time, though, I found myself not quite able to dismiss it either.

I tried to estimate the likelihood of another person looking like Kenny. It seemed remote, but I had heard of such "twins" before, men who could step into the shoes of their doubles and successfully impersonate them. I thought I remembered reading about a spy from the World War II era who had done just that.

Was this what had happened to us? Was this young man only an impostor, who looked so much like Kenny that he had dared to come into his home and attempt to deceive us? There were times during the days that followed when this possibility seemed to me more and more likely. I found myself watching Kenny constantly, studying him as unobtrusively as I could, and at times he seemed not at all like Kenny, as though he really were another person altogether.

If this were the case, it would explain a great deal that had puzzled me since Kenny's return. It would account for all the slips: calling me Ingemar instead of Mar, ignoring the intimacy that had once existed between us. An impostor might have forgotten the nickname, and couldn't possibly know about the other.

"Or maybe you're just soothing your ego," I would argue with myself. It was no less possible that Kenny, excited to be home, might have slipped on the name. Memory told me that he had called me Ingemar a time or two when we were kids, when he was affecting a stuffy formal manner, trying to be funny. I had forgotten about that on the day he arrived home. So, he wasn't the only one to forget things. As for the other, the intimacy we had shared, well, he might have forgotten all about that or, more likely, he might have chosen to ignore it as boyhood foolishness.

There were times when some gesture, some little word, convinced me after all that I must be crazy to think that this wasn't really Kenny, no matter how much he had changed, or forgotten. There weren't more than a handful of minor details to indicate otherwise, and on the other hand, there was no end of evidence that Kenny was genuine. I told myself this time and time again, but still the questions nagged at me.

If a man could devise a seed that would grow as fast and with such a bountiful harvest as the seed of suspicion, he'd no doubt make a fortune for himself. The seed had been planted in my mind and it grew—at first underground, so that I wasn't really aware how strong it was becoming, or how deep its roots had reached.

Soon enough, however, it broke the surface and began to spread across my mind. I found myself thinking more and more about the scrap of paper that I had seen, with Kenny's name written on it, again and again, in an uncertain and changing manner. What about the letter from Ingrid to Douglas Allen, I asked myself repeatedly? Who was he, anyway, and what did he have to do with all this?

For that matter, what about Ingrid herself? She'd been in Indianapolis, attending school. She had written to someone there after she came back and, soon after that, Kenny had written from somewhere in Indiana. Where exactly had it come from, his letter? I tried to remember, and realized I didn't know. I had never seen that letter myself, except in Ingrid's hands, while she read it. For that matter, so far as I could recall, no one else had seen it, except Ingrid.

Of course, Ingrid hadn't mentioned that the letter seemed in any way questionable. Surely she would have noticed if the handwriting wasn't Kenny's. And, it stood to reason, if that letter had come from Kenny, then the man who was here had to be Kenny.

Unless, of course, the letter hadn't come from Kenny, and Ingrid hadn't commented on the handwriting for the simple reason that she knew in advance that it wasn't Kenny's

There was a considerable amount of wealth tied up in Mrs. Baker's estate. Probably, if you totaled it all up, the farm, the other properties, furnishings and equipment, what was in the bank, it would run somewhere more than a million dollars. Certainly it was enough to have set Ingrid scheming, and Kenny himself, for that matter. From one scheme to another, it seemed, was only a short step. If it was likely that Kenny and Ingrid were scheming, in a small way, to get the farm and the properties, was it any less reasonable that Ingrid and an impostor might be scheming on a larger scale?

If Kenny and Ingrid were involved in some such scheme, they must have realized how close they had come to giving themselves away. Kenny's accident on a horse could have aroused someone else's suspicions as well as mine.

And for all I knew, they might have discovered that I had opened that dresser drawer and seen its contents. Had I even remembered to replace them properly? I couldn't remember and had no chance of checking.

It seemed to me, though, that their manner had changed, not only toward one another, but toward me as well. I found myself more and more aware of that strange watchfulness of Ingrid's, but it seemed now as though it wasn't only Kenny whom she was watching. I had the feeling that she was watching me too, watching for any sign of doubt or suspicion. Several times, when we found ourselves alone together for a minute or so, I thought Ingrid was on the verge of broaching the subject. She would seem as though she were about to speak, but each time she was sidetracked—either someone else would approach and prevent any such conversation, or she herself would seem to have a change of heart.

On the other hand, I might have been imagining it, and the feeling I had that she was watching me and weighing me in the balance may have been nothing more than the fruits of my suspicions.

As for Kenny, he went through a period where, probably because of his wounded pride, he acted sulky and kept himself somewhat aloof from the rest of us. Gradually, his usual good spirits—that is, usual for Kenny—returned.

Strangely enough, I thought I detected a difference in his attitude toward Ingrid. They were still together a lot, and there was still a surface appearance of affection and even romance, but it did not seem to me to ring true. There were times when, although Kenny agreed quickly enough to Ingrid's suggestions that they go to such and such a place together, it seemed that he was reluctant. From time to time I would see him go off someplace by himself and when I later observed Ingrid looking around for him, I would realize he had slipped off without saying anything to her.

Yet as much as these things seemed to support my suspicions, I had to admit that they could as easily prove that Kenny was genuine. It was the way he would have acted. If he had taken a spill on a horse, as he had done plenty of times in the past, he was always out of spirits for a day or two; and Kenny had never liked being tied to anyone's apron strings. He had always liked to get off by himself at times.

So it went, back and forth in my mind. But there was one thing that did become apparent, enough so that I could be sure I was not imagining it. Kenny had undergone a change as a result of his accident, or at least after the accident, whatever the cause. Whether he was an impostor and he had realized that I suspected him, or whether he really was Kenny and had other reasons, he began gradually to become friendlier toward me.

It wasn't anything that happened all at once, of course. No matter how genuine he might have been, or how sincere his motives, we had built a lot of walls between us, walls that did not come down easily. For the first time since his return, though, Kenny made a move in my direction. If I could have been sure of the reasons for it, I think I'd have been the happiest man alive, but I couldn't help suspecting him and everything that he did now, and as a result I was only more miserable with every approach that he made.

The first time came as a surprise, although it was a relatively minor matter. I never had gotten out to check that fence the day of Kenny's accident. By the time I had seen to him, and gotten the Jeep running again, it was too late in the day, and I'd had other business to attend to since.

It was almost a week later that I mentioned to Olsen at breakfast that I was on my way out to look over the work that had been done, just to assure myself that it was satisfactory. Like any farm, we had a few hands whose work was only as good as the eye you kept on them.

Kenny was with us in the kitchen that morning. He frequently was, although not as constantly as had been true in the past. To my surprise, he asked if he could join me.

"You know, I haven't seen much of this place since I've been back," he said. "Funny, at one time I think I knew every clod of dirt on the place, and now I feel like a stranger to it."

At first I was as pleased as punch, and I made him welcome to come with me. As I thought about it later, though, I began to wonder again. If he were an impostor, there was a great deal that Ingrid couldn't have told him. She wasn't much of a farmer, after all. There were things he would have to learn from someone more familiar with that part of Kenny's past. Someone like me. I cursed myself for wondering, for not being able to accept his offer of friendship at face value—but I couldn't, and by the time we were in the Jeep and headed across the fields, I had become gloomy and non-talkative.

"We haven't seen much of one another since I got back," he said, trying to break the thick silence that had fallen between us.

"We've been living in the same house," I answered him, but though I tried to make it sound casual, he had succeeded in parting the curtain of gloom, at least a little, and my heart beat faster. I waited for him to go on, hoping that he might make some comment, however small, about the way things had been between us in the past. I had more than one reason for wanting to hear it. If he remembered at all, if he knew anything about what had gone on between us, he could only be Kenny. No one else had known about that.

"I didn't remember us being so busy." He was silent for a while, looking around at the bundles of corn shocks and the stubble of cut grain. "I've forgotten a lot, Mar," he said finally. "And there are other things I remember as clearly as though they were last week. Funny, the things a man forgets, and the things he remembers."

That was all he said, and it told me nothing. He might have been hinting, looking for some sign from me that I hadn't forgotten—or he might have been trying to convince me of who he was, and explaining away his mistakes. I didn't know which.

There was one other thing that happened that same day, while Kenny and I were together, something that I had been expecting all along and waiting for apprehensively. Kenny and Dexter met, for the first time in five years.

They didn't exactly meet, that is to say, they only saw one another. We were at the fence and the job that had been done on it was quite a bit short of the best fencing I had ever seen. Cussing under my breath, I set about tightening up the wires and straightening some of the posts. Kenny helped me. I didn't ask and he didn't offer, he just started in working when I did. He took to it naturally. If he was a fake, he at least had been raised somewhere where they put up fences.

It's a habit of mine that I lose myself in my work. When I'm really busy at something, I don't pay much attention to anything else, even to whether someone else is working or not. I don't know how long it was after Kenny had stopped working that I noticed. When I did, I looked up to see him staring into the distance beyond our fence. Before I even followed the direction of his gaze, I guessed what he was staring at. The fence marked the boundary between our farm and Dexter Holloman's.

When I looked up, I saw Dexter. He was still a hundred yards or more away, walking slowly toward us. Kenny must have watched him come all the way across an acre of open field.

He saw that I was looking too. "That's Holloman, isn't it?" he asked, still watching the approaching figure.

He might have recognized Dexter, or he might simply have known that the adjoining field was Holloman's. "Yes," was all I said.

Holloman was close enough to see plainly now. Not that my memory needed refreshing. I saw him usually once a month or so, in passing. That was as much as I wanted to see of him. I had wondered sometimes if Kenny had ever told Holloman about me. Once or twice it had seemed as though Holloman were trying very hard to be friendly, or as though his manner toward me were conspiratorial.

I wasn't having any, not then or now. I suppose he was good looking enough, in an unmanly way. He had a lot of flash and polish that I supposed came from rubbing elbows in places like Chicago. He was showing his age, which must have been well past forty by this time, but he carried it well. In the past, when things had been happening between him and Kenny, there were plenty of people who had considered Holloman downright handsome. For myself, I could see he was the sort of character a boy might like—a man wouldn't, but a boy might.

He'd seen us looking in his direction and he waved at us. It was plain that he was coming to see us. I didn't flatter myself that it was me who had attracted him. I looked at

Kenny, but I couldn't read his face—it was perfectly blank, although his eyes never moved from the approaching figure.

"I think we're finished here," I said on an impulse, gathering up the tools with a deliberate nonchalance.

Kenny looked at me. He knew as well as I did that we had another's hour's work. I thought he was going to point that out, or tell me to mind my own business. He didn't though. He simply nodded and started toward the Jeep with me. As he climbed into it, he waved back in the direction of Holloman, who had come to a stop when we walked away.

I didn't wait for Kenny to change his mind. We put up a cloud of dust as I turned the Jeep around sharply and started back toward the house.

CHAPTER ELEVEN

I couldn't tell just what effect the sight of Dexter had had on Kenny. He was subdued on the way back to the house, and I felt that I had made my feelings on that score clear enough with our hasty departure, without making any comments about it.

Even at that, I had interfered. I was the last person who had any right to tell Kenny not to see the man if he wanted to. Whether he wanted to or not, he didn't say. He gave no sign that he was annoyed by my butting in, but at the same time, he seemed distant afterward, wrapped up in thoughts of his own. If he was Kenny, he was probably remembering. Some of those memories must have been pleasant. If he wasn't Kenny, he'd have a lot to think about, deciding how to handle this development.

Ingrid was on the porch when we got back. She came out to meet us. She seemed cheerful enough, but I thought she gave me a less than affectionate look as she latched onto Kenny's arm.

"You're nasty," she scolded him with a mock pout. "I had so many plans for you today and here you are running off with Mar and looking at silly fences."

"It's about time I started doing some work," he answered as they moved off toward the house. "If I keep up the way I have been, I'll get fat and lazy."

They moved out of my range of hearing, still talking to one another, but in lower voices. I watched them, Ingrid clinging to his arm, Kenny; slowing his pace to match hers. His lean hips had a lazy rhythm, rising and falling as he sprang forward on his toes with each step, the natural walk of a young Indian.

Lazy, maybe, I found myself thinking, but whoever he was, he'd be a long time getting fat.

If Kenny was sore because I had dragged him away from Holloman, he got over it apparently by the next day. I had planned on going into town, and again he suggested going with me. I didn't mind, even if I couldn't take his overtures at face value. At least he was spending a little time with me, and despite all my suspicions and my resentments, I was glad to have him at my side. If he wasn't Kenny, he was enough like him that he continued to stir up all the old feelings, and the old torments, inside me.

It was an uneventful trip and, just as the day before, we did little talking. Kenny stayed with me while I tended to business, paying attention but offering little in the way of comment or interference. Either he had learned a little tact while he was gone, or he was being cautious.

What little conversation there was, was general and vague, and anything but personal, until we came back to the farm. I stopped the car at the road, just as we pulled onto the dirt and gravel of the drive.

"Looks like the mail's come," I told him. "May as well take that up to the house and save Pete a hike down here."

He got out and went around the car to the mailbox, opening it to take out a small handful of letters. As he started back to the car, he flipped through them, and stopped abruptly, holding one of the letters apart from the others. Still standing where he was, he tore it open and read it through quickly.

At first, he appeared surprised and puzzled. As he read, his face turned angry. He finished the letter and, with a rough gesture, he crumpled it into a ball and threw it into the ditch. Tightlipped, he came back to the car, tossing the other mail onto the seat between us as he slid inside.

I didn't ask about the letter. I didn't have to. I was sure I knew who had written it, and I was glad for one thing at least: Kenny had seemed surprised, and upset, to receive a letter from Dexter.

He said nothing until we were almost to the house. When he spoke, his words caught me off guard. "Don't shut me out, Mar," he said out of a clear blue sky. "Give me a chance, at least."

"At what?" I asked stupidly.

"At what I came back for."

I glanced briefly in his direction. He was staring across the seat at me, but I couldn't decipher the expression on his face. He looked sad and anxious, as though he were trying to reach me in some way.

I realized finally that he was talking about the farm. That was what he had come back for, after all. "It's got nothing to do with me," I said. "Besides, I don't think there's much doubt that you'll end up owning the place."

We had arrived at the house by this time. I pulled up in front and switched off the engine. When I looked at him, I knew I'd said the wrong thing. He was puzzled and disappointed. I suppose he had meant to enlist my help in their schemes, but as strong as the hold was that he had on me, I meant to stay out of that business. I couldn't fight him, but I wouldn't join him, either.

"We'd better go in," I said, since he was just sitting there without moving, not looking at me but staring though the windshield as if watching some drama that only he could see being performed. "Supper will be ready pretty soon."

I found myself thinking a great deal about the letter that Kenny had received from Holloman. I even came close to going back to the road and looking for it where Kenny had tossed it, but I couldn't quite bring myself to that sort of snooping. Even if Kenny were really who he claimed to be, it was none of my business what he did or didn't do with Holloman. At the same time, even if he were someone else, I couldn't help feeling jealous and resentful.

I was sure, too, that throwing the letter away hadn't helped Kenny to forget it either. He had been angry at first, perhaps because of Holloman's sheer gall, or perhaps because this development meant new problems for him, but he had begun to feel the draw of the personality that had once brought so much unhappiness into this house.

Regardless of my own dislike for the man, Holloman seemed to exercise a considerable influence over those who fell under his spell. Kenny was feeling it now, I was sure. I could see that in his newly acquired restlessness. It was a trait of the old Kenny, the way he had acted in the past, when he wanted to do something that he knew damn well he shouldn't. It was how I had usually known in the past when Kenny was up to something. This time, unlike many another, I knew what it was Kenny was up to, and I waited and watched anxiously to see whether or not he would succumb to the temptation.

I think during this period I was truly convinced of Kenny's identity. I had ceased to think of him as "whoever," and when he was on my mind, which was nearly all the time, I thought of him simply as Kenny. For the time being I had put aside my suspicions, but this was nothing striking. Since I had first formed them, I had done the same thing a dozen times or more, only to have them come back stronger and more fully developed than before.

* * * * * * *

"Did you and Kenny have a quarrel about something?" Olsen asked one afternoon.

"What makes you think that?" I asked. I hadn't stopped to think that we might give that impression. Like most people, although I had been aware of Kenny's nervousness, I hadn't thought for a minute that mine might be equally obvious.

"You've both been as jumpy as all get out," she said. "I'm almost afraid to say anything to either of you."

"We've got nothing to quarrel about," I told her, which wasn't exactly an answer to her question, but she let it go at that.

I was surprised when Ingrid, too, approached me about the difficulty and came very close to echoing Olsen's question.

102

"What's wrong between you and Kenny?" Hers was a typically direct approach.

"Should something be?" I countered. But it was odd that they should both link Kenny and me together the way they did. It didn't seem to me that a quarrel between us would be a very logical explanation for his behavior. Of all the things that might upset him, I was certainly the least likely, as I saw it.

I didn't for a moment suspect that Dexter Holloman would be put off so easily, and he wasn't. There were other letters. I couldn't say how many, because I never saw any that might have come the times Kenny went for the mail himself, but I saw Pete hand him at least two others. Holloman was pleading his case, apparently, and with each new letter, I saw Kenny's indecision and nervousness increasing. Something was going to give, I was sure of that, and soon.

Strangely enough, much as I disliked Holloman and resented him, I couldn't help feeling a bit sorry for him. I knew what he must be going through. He was alone now in that big old house down the road, and I could picture him sitting there, maybe pacing the floor, waiting and wondering, almost afraid to hope.

Unlike mine, Holloman's prayers were answered.

* * * * * * *

The early winter that Olsen had predicted had arrived during this time. The evening that Kenny had received the first letter, we'd had flurries of snow that fell in timid wisps and melted a minute or two after it touched the ground.

A few nights later it came again with more confidence and we awoke in the morning to the sight of a thin blanket of whiteness over the ground. The wind swept over the fields, reminding us that there was more to come, and the pear tree outside my window stretched her branches to scrape lightly against the house, as though asking to come inside where it was warm.

From my room, where to be honest with myself I usually lay at night and strained my ears to keep track of Kenny, I could often hear him moving about below. He would pace the floor before the fireplace, pause for a while, and then resume his impatient pacing. My body ached with the desire to go down to him, but fear held me back. With each passing day, with each sight of him and every word he spoke to me, I felt the reins that held my emotions in check grow tauter.

One night I fell asleep only to be awakened some time later. The house seemed still, but I lifted my head from the pillow, trying to remember what it was that had brought me out of sleep. Some sound, apparently, but I couldn't remember.

I was almost convinced I had imagined it, and had dropped my head back to the pillow to return to sleep, when I heard another sound, this time from below. It seemed to come from the front porch. I got up and moved across the room, the bare floor icy cold on my feet.

Outside, the night seemed innocent and calm. There was a quarter moon, its pale light enhanced by the fresh snow that covered the ground and the trees with a ghostly whiteness. For a moment I saw nothing, and then there was a flicker of movement, little more than a shadow, that disturbed the other, unmoving shadows of the trees and the buildings. Someone, or something, was there, slipping through the protective darkness where I could see only faint hints of an alien presence.

I thought of the prowlers that had been mentioned once or twice around town. This might be perfectly innocent—a stray dog looking for a scrap of food, or something equally harmless. Or it might also be a prowler. There was only one way to find out. I slipped quickly into a pair of jeans and my shoes, and as I crept out into the hall I was buttoning up a shirt. I started for the stairs, and stopped to think. If there were any trouble, it would be foolish to leave the people in the house unaware and unsuspecting. The likelihood of anything serious happening was slim, but there nonetheless.

Without thinking of the estrangement between us, I went back along the hall to Kenny's room. A knock at his door might have also aroused the women, so instead I merely opened the door and stuck my head inside, calling his name in a whisper. There was no reply. I went into the room, to his bed, thinking to shake him awake. There was no need for that, however.

The bed was empty.

* * * * * * *

Kenny had forgotten that snow, for all that it conceals, can be revealing as well. His footprints stood out clearly where they left the cleanness of the walk and headed across the yard. I stepped into the yard after them, but I followed them only a short distance. Kenny was far away by this time, and his trail confirmed what I had already guessed. It led straight off in the direction of Holloman. I went back to my room.

The sky was turning gray with the approach of dawn when I heard Kenny return, stealing back into the house as stealthily as he had gone.

Not until then did I sleep again.

Kenny's Back, by Victor J. Banis

CHAPTER TWELVE

Looking back on those days, it seems as though I spent them jumping back and forth from one conviction to another, with no comfort to be found in either. Either Kenny was who he seemed to be, and I was being foolish and even disloyal to suspect him, or he was not Kenny at all, and I was being slow to accept that fact.

In actuality, it wasn't quite that way. I believed in Kenny, because I wanted to believe in him. I'd waited a long time for him to come back, and I wasn't eager to send him away again. At the same time, the doubts came and went, tormenting me and adding a peculiar confusion to everything that happened. It was as though I was seeing double. Everything that happened had two sides to it, two possible sets of explanations.

The fact that he had gone to Dexter might have meant that the man in the house was Kenny, and that the lure of the past had been too strong for him to resist, but that wasn't a realization that I found particularly comforting.

On the other hand, an impostor, concerned by the increasing pressure Holloman was apparently applying, might have feared being exposed by Holloman. If he were really worried, he might try to bluff the threat out, by going to Holloman and convincing him of the deception—but this reasoning brought me back to the prospect of a fake Kenny, and I didn't much like that conclusion either.

All this while, though, I was stubbornly ignoring one simple fact: if I'd really had the confidence that I tried to convince myself I had in Kenny's authenticity, it would have been a fairly easy matter to prove, and once and for all to satisfy the nagging doubts. There were ways in which I could have tested Kenny, things that I could have asked him about that no impostor, however clever, could have known.

The truth is, however, that by the time I had allowed myself to consider asking these question, I had lost my confidence in Kenny's authenticity, and since I couldn't bring myself to answer the questions banging around in my head, I chose the only alternative: I tried to ignore them. For a short time, I nearly succeeded, but they were brought back to me again by a fairly harmless comment that came from Pete. It was the only part Pete was to play in our little drama, but it was a decisive one so far as I was concerned.

If the truth were told, Pete did not really have a great deal to do around the place, not enough at any rate to keep him busy. Nor was this any matter of charity. He had worked on the farm for many years, since before I had come there, and if he wasn't too bright about a lot of things, and a bit testy, he was also honest and a good worker. He had earned his state of semi-retirement, a decision in which Mrs. Baker had wholeheartedly concurred when I had brought the matter up with her.

For several years I had gradually cut down Pete's duties, replacing some of them with lighter work, small chores he could perform around the house. He also occupied himself with making a little moonshine, and some dandelion wine. Pete and I mostly kept the knowledge of the moonshine to ourselves, for obvious reasons, but the wine was general knowledge, and even Olsen, who sniffed and pretended to disapprove of this particular hobby, had to begrudgingly admit that a glass of his dandelion wine produced a very pleasant mood on a winter's evening. Each year Mrs. Baker gave a few bottles of that around as Christmas gifts to friends and neighbors, and they were always happily received.

The moonshine, Pete kept for himself. Apparently I ranked well enough in his opinion, however, as I was from time to time invited to stop at his shack for a drink out of the bottle in which he kept his "running stock."

I wasn't much of a drinker, but I liked the old man. When you could get him started, he had many an interesting yarn to spin. I wouldn't have wanted to swear to the truth of some of them, but they made good listening. There were worse ways to spend an evening than sitting in the shack, next to the old coal burning stove that he insisted on retaining, drinking White Lightning and listening to his stories. As he talked, Pete would help himself to a chew. He was always polite enough to offer me some, but only because he knew that I'd decline. As he talked, rambling on without expecting much in the way of reply, he would spit in the general direction of the large can he kept near the door, which as often as not, he missed.

This had been a busy autumn and I hadn't had many such evenings. I guess I missed them in a vague way, without knowing just what it was that was missing. On the day after Kenny's nighttime trip across the fields, I saw Pete in the barn, and he extended his offhand invitation.

"Got some good stuff this year," he informed me, just as though he were commenting on the weather. "You oughta stop by some night and have a drink. It'll put hair on your chest."

Pete had been promising hair on my chest for almost ten years, with little results, but the memory of his warm stove and the strong liquor struck me as very inviting and a welcome relief from the way things were around the house.

"I just might be out tonight," I decided aloud. "If you've got nothing better to do."

I had half expected that Kenny's trip to Holloman's place would have at least accomplished one thing, of relieving his nervous melancholy. Surprisingly enough, however, that seemed to have gone worse by the next morning, and he went around the house all that day with a mile-long face.

I wasn't exactly in the best of spirits myself. What with the two of us moping around, and Ingrid's worried face, the house had all the cheer of a funeral parlor. I was really glad to slip out the back door during the evening and make my way back to the shack where Pete was heaping up the fire and alternately cursing the red-glowing stove.

"If you weren't so contrary you could have some real heat out here," I reminded him. "Mrs. Baker wanted this place changed over three years ago."

"Damn oil and gas heaters," he snorted. His shot at the can came close to staining my overalls. "Wouldn't have them. You've got them in the house and you still have to build a fire every night to keep the frost off things."

It was a long standing argument, and although I had explained many times that we had fires in the fireplace for the pleasure of them rather than out of necessity, Pete was no more likely to give up his little coal stove than he was going to stop making his home brews.

"Here, this'll warm you up," he said, shoving his bottle at me. I gave him a salute with it and tried a swallow. It tasted just about the way kerosene smelled, and I wouldn't have been surprised to learn that it came by that flavor honestly.

"Not bad," I told him, trying to ignore the fire moving from my mouth down toward my stomach. He was right about one thing: it warmed you up. "I liked last year's better."

"Last year's?" He gave a disdainful snort. "That was like worm juice. This here is good liquor."

He testified to the fact by turning the bottle up and drinking down a hearty mouthful before handing it back to me. We settled in the two chairs in front of the stove and I propped by feet up on a wooden crate full of coal. Burning or not, the White Lightning had done what nothing else had been able to do lately: it had put me in a cozy mood.

"I heard there was a bobcat over on the Patterson place," Pete said. "Think I'll load up the gun and have it handy, in case it heads this way."

I thought at once of Kenny's midnight journey. "Maybe I ought to mention it to Kenny," I said. "He always liked tracking them down. Save you shooting Olsen some night when she takes the garbage out."

"She ain't likely to be traipsin' around in the middle of the night like a bobcat," he said. "If you want to know, I heard something last night. I got my gun out, but by the time I got outside there wasn't nothing in sight. Reckon it heard me stirring. Next time, though, I'll be ready for him."

So Pete had heard Kenny, or else me, walking around erasing Kenny's tracks. His hearing was better than his eyesight, it seemed. It looked as though I'd have to find some way of warning Kenny to keep clear of Pete's shack if he was planning on going out at night.

"Anyhow," Pete went on, not about to back down on an argument, "I don't know it would do any good to mention it to him."

"Why not? Kenny's always liked hunting, and he was pretty good with a gun, too." I accepted the bottle from him again and lifted it to take another drink.

"He ain't Kenny."

I nearly dropped the bottle, which would have been like cutting off Pete's leg. My hands were shaking, and I balanced the bottle on my knee instead of taking the drink I had intended.

"What makes you say that?" I asked, trying to sound normal.

"He's changed, that's all. He ain't the old Kenny anymore. That's what living among strangers does for you, it makes a different person out of you."

I took the drink then, feeling like I needed it. I knew Pete better than to think he was being subtle, or dropping any hints. He meant no more nor less than what he said—that Kenny was a different person—but his words so closely echoed my fears, like hearing my thoughts voiced, that I found myself facing those thoughts again, and squarely this time, and suddenly I knew that I could no longer ignore them. I had to know the truth, no matter what it cost me.

* * * * * * *

The house was already still when I returned from Pete's shack. I debated about dropping in on Kenny in his room, and drawing him into a conversation. The circumstances would make it easy to steer the conversation into the right channels. But I thought, too, that Kenny might be asleep by this time. He hadn't gotten much sleep the night before, I reminded myself. Worse yet, he might be preparing for another trip to Holloman's. I didn't feel I was quite up to facing that yet.

In the end, I went to my own room, deciding to wait for the right opportunity to present itself. I remembered Pete and his gun, which he had made a point of getting out and loading before I left his place. A fear that Kenny might be going out again tonight kept me awake into the small hours of the morning. The house remained silent, however, and I fell asleep at last, sure by this time that Kenny must be asleep too.

Afterward, I was to regret not taking advantage of that opportunity to talk to Kenny. I had no way of knowing, of course, how close we were to a turning point, and by the time another opportunity presented itself to me, things had changed greatly.

There was one other event that took place during this same time and that was to have a considerable effect on what followed.

I was slow in appreciating the tightrope that Ingrid was walking. From Kenny's standpoint, it seemed as though he had accomplished his objective. With each passing day, he was more securely installed in his position and, from all indications, he could look forward to being a wealthy man in the not-too-distant future.

Ingrid's work was still cut out for her. She had given whatever help she could to Kenny and, thus far, she had no rewards of her own. She stood to gain from her efforts only through Kenny, through marrying him. Until she had accomplished that, Kenny was master of the place, and she was still just a hired hand.

Ingrid was intelligent enough that she must have seen this from the beginning. She was gambling, it seemed, on her ability to charm Kenny into falling in love with her. Or else, she had some power over him great enough to force him to her way of thinking—such as the knowledge that he was a fake.

Ingrid wasted no time in making her plans evident. How much of them she had discussed with Kenny beforehand I had no way of knowing. I know that he was surprised by what she did next, although he certainly must have expected something of the sort.

It happened the day after my visit to Pete's shack. Ingrid was the last to come in to supper that evening, and she looked flushed and excited as she took her place at the table. She had on a white dress, with a ribbon holding her blonde hair back from her face, and around her neck she had tied a brightly colored scarf. Ordinarily I wouldn't have noticed any of this, and I probably wouldn't have this time either except that Olsen called my attention to Ingrid's appearance.

I saw the shocked look she gave Ingrid as my sister sat down at the table. Until Olsen spoke, which was not for a full minute, I couldn't understand the reason for her surprise.

"That's Mrs. Baker's scarf," she said finally, coming around the table to stare wide-eyed at Ingrid.

It was the first I had noticed the scarf. Now that I did, though, I recognized it at once. It had come from Italy, where Mrs. Baker and her husband had gone on their honeymoon, and many was the time she had proudly displayed the souvenir to friends while she talked wistfully of the places she had seen and the things she had done.

Ingrid did not look at all perturbed. If anything, she looked pleased that the scarf had been noticed. "Yes," she answered, fingering the silk proudly, "Kenny gave it to me. It's an engagement present," she added before anyone else had a chance to speak.

Kenny must have had a real time of it to keep from blowing his lid. He managed to look calm, and he finally got a weak smile on his face, but it was lucky for him that Olsen was too surprised herself and excited by this news to notice his bewilderment. I was sure that this was also the first that Kenny knew he had proposed to Ingrid.

"Ingrid, Kenny, how wonderful!" Olsen exclaimed, beside herself with delight.

Kenny and I were the only two, it seemed, who were less than enthusiastic, and he managed a better job of pretending than I did.

"We planned to surprise you with it," he said lamely. I didn't point out that, as a surprise, it had been pretty successful anyway, for everyone, including him.

"Mar?" Olsen finally noticed my silence for the first time. "Aren't you going to congratulate them?"

"Sure," I said. Olsen couldn't see my face as I looked at the two of them, but neither Ingrid nor Kenny were likely to have any doubts about my feelings on the matter. "Congratulations. On everything."

I looked from one to the other of the pair, and all of my suspicions must have been plain to see in my face. Ingrid met my look with a haughty one of her own and with no lessening of her self-satisfied smile—but Kenny wilted and looked away.

Without speaking a word, I had made my accusations—and they, just as silently, had admitted their guilt.

CHAPTER THIRTEEN

For two or three nights after Kenny's visit to Hollo-man, I slept with one eye open and my ears cocked for some indication of another trip. I had managed to accomplish one thing, and that was to let Kenny know, offhandedly, that I was aware of what he had done. To everyone else, my re-mark probably sounded fully innocent, but I knew that he would get the message.

"Pete thought he heard a bobcat last night," I said, "He's loaded up his gun in case it comes around again."

It was all I said on the subject, and I made it as casual sounding as I could, but I gave Kenny a warning look as I said it. I was sure from his expression that he understood what I was telling him. In concentrating my attention on Kenny, however, I missed one other face: someone else had understood the meaning hidden within that remark also.

Four nights after his first trip, Kenny went out again. I heard his door close softly and the sound of stealthy foot-steps along the hall. It seemed to me that he paused very briefly at my door, but it was so brief that I might have imag-ined it altogether. The footsteps disappeared down the hall and I heard the front door a moment or two later.

I sat up in bed and started for the window to see if Kenny would be careful to avoid Pete's shack. Before I reached the window, though, something happened that made me stop and listen. Another door had opened and closed quietly, and once again there were muffled footsteps going past my door.

Olsen? It was possible that she had heard the noises and was on her way to investigate, but Olsen wasn't a foolish or a reckless woman. If it was her, she would stop at my room to tell me she had heard something.

These steps, however, went by my room without pause, and I was sure then that it wasn't Olsen making her way along the hall to the stairs. I went to the window, looking down on the stillness below. Kenny was nowhere in sight. He'd had time enough to disappear on his way. Apparently he'd heeded my warning, or else Pete had slept soundly.

A moment later, someone did appear. Unlike Kenny, Ingrid did not think to remain in the shadows, but stepped straight off the porch into the moonlight. She looked down at the ground, probably at footprints, although at my distance it was hard to distinguish between the marks in the snow.

I saw her look up, staring in the direction of the barn. She started toward it and then veered off, and I guessed she was following Kenny's trail. At the corner of the barn, she stopped again, staring into the distance. Kenny had avoided Pete's shack, it seemed, and circled around the barn before heading across the fields.

Ingrid came back to the house, rubbing her arms against the night's chill. I remained where I was for a moment or two, looking away in the direction that Kenny had gone, as though my eyes might penetrate the night and pick him out as he made his way over the crusted snow.

I was still at the window when Ingrid came from the house again. She had put on a coat and scarf, and now she started off again in the direction of the barn. My mind was filled with all sorts of anxieties. I didn't much care for the thought of Ingrid traipsing around alone at night, apparently headed for Holloman's. For all I knew, there really might be a bobcat prowling between our place and his.

Even if the fields and woods held no danger for her, there was the question of what would happen when she arrived. I had seen how Holloman took to being caught in the act. If he could rough up one woman, his own wife, he would

116

probably do the same to Ingrid. Kenny would be there, of course, but I wasn't any too sure what difference that might make.

As it turned out, my fears on that score were unnecessary. Ingrid wasn't going to follow Kenny after all. Instead, she went straight to the barn, disappearing through the little door that hung in the larger one. It seemed as if she meant to wait for Kenny's return.

From my window I had a better view than Ingrid had. Beyond the barn I could see a large section of the moonlit pasture that he would have to cross coming home. I would see him returning long before she would hear his footsteps on the hardened snow.

A full two hours had passed before I caught the first glimpse of him. He was walking fast across the pasture. Then he passed out of my sight. Still not sure what it was I intended to do, I left my room and, as Kenny and Ingrid had both done earlier, stole downstairs.

Unlike them, I went out the back way. I was still worried about Pete and his gun. If Ingrid and Kenny started a commotion, I didn't want Pete mistaking them for prowlers or bobcats.

I headed for his shack first. I thought, as I tapped at his door, that he might just as easily think I was a prowler and shoot before he opened the door. I was thankful when I heard his voice, demanding to know who was there.

"It's Mar," I told him as softly as I could. "Be quiet and open up."

He opened the door, but my whisper must not have sounded for certain like my ordinary voice, because the shotgun came out first.

"What's happening?" he asked after he had convinced himself that it was really me.

"Nothing important," I told him, "But I was up and I didn't want you mistaking me for a bobcat."

"Is there any trouble?" He looked past me at the yard, which, thankfully, was still empty. He hadn't been kidding about keeping the gun ready, either. It was loaded and cocked.

"Nothing to worry about," I assured him. "Just don't go using that thing if you hear any noises, okay?"

He looked a little puzzled, which was understandable, but he nodded and with some reluctance went back inside. As I started across the yard in the direction of the barn, I was glad I had taken the time to alert him. One of the horses whinnied. Kenny was apparently on his way around the barn. It was the sort of noise that would have been sure to bring Pete out shooting.

Ingrid had guessed what that noise meant, too. She came out of the barn and only the fact that I was in the shadow of the pear tree kept her from seeing me. I froze, afraid to risk attracting attention by moving for cover, but Ingrid wasn't looking in my direction. She went straight for the corner of the barn and reached it at almost the same time as Kenny.

He jumped and nearly let her have it with his fist before he recognized her. I could pretty well imagine how surprised he was to meet her there, in the middle of the night.

They were too far away for me to hear their conversation. From the looks of it, they were having sharp words. Ingrid tugged at his sleeve. Kenny pulled away once, but the second time he gave in and reluctantly followed her to the barn. They disappeared inside, leaving me alone in the yard.

Two thoughts crossed my mind. The first was that I had no business being here. It didn't look as though there was going to be anything more serious than a quarrel, and my excuse that I was worried for Ingrid's sake no longer held water.

The second thought was that this might be my best chance to learn the answers to the questions that were troubling me. With some misgivings, I chose the second possibility. Promising myself that I would go back to bed if there was nothing going on but a lover's quarrel, I moved toward the barn, picking my way carefully so as not to make any more noise than was necessary.

The barn, while better built than some, nonetheless had an ample number of openings and cracks in the walls. It wasn't hard to find a place outside from which I could see in and observe them. When I saw them, there was little question that a quarrel was in progress. Just now, though, Ingrid and Kenny didn't impress me as lovers.

Their voices came and went. Both of them were trying to be quiet, and some of the conversation was in a whisper, but at the same time both of them had their dander up, and their voices kept going up with it.

"I'll do what I damn well please," I heard Kenny say. His face was livid with anger. It was plain he didn't like being followed.

"You damn fool." Ingrid was in no better spirits herself. I don't think I had ever seen her like this, her face an ugly mask that had little resemblance to the sweet girl I was used to. It was the first time I had heard her swear, too. I was seeing a part of Ingrid that I had never known existed.

I missed some more of it, until they started raising their voices again. Ingrid was berating him for something: "…taking chances like that. Don't you realize he's the one person who could give us away?"

Her next words, barely audible, broke on my ears like a clap of thunder: "He's the one person who would know you're not Kenny."

I didn't hear his answer, not because he was speaking too low, but because Ingrid's words were still ringing in my ears. For a minute or two, everything else was blotted out. All I could think of was that he was not Kenny. My suspicions, which had seemed too incredible to believe, had been proven after all.

He was speaking when I began to listen again. "Holloman didn't seem to mind," he said with an unpleasant sneer on his face. For the first time I was seeing how he really felt toward Ingrid. For all that pretended romance and affection, the look on his face at this moment told me that he must hate her very much. Right now he wasn't trying to hide it. "He didn't act like he had any suspicions, either," he finished.

She said something I didn't hear, at which he only laughed. With an angry toss of her head, she turned away from him as though to leave.

"I'm warning you," she said to him over her shoulder.

He caught her hand in a quick, rough movement, almost jerking her off her feet. There was fear on her face as she looked up at him.

"I know what's bothering you," he said. He pulled her close into his arms, against his body. "You're jealous of him. You want what he's getting, don't you?"

"You're crazy," she told him, struggling to get away from him, "Let go of me."

She wasn't any match for him. He held her with no effort and grinned at her attempts to escape him. "Maybe I ought to give it to you," he said.

"No." The rest of her protest was cut off as he kissed her, hard. He stepped forward, carrying her easily with him. They were in front of an empty stall. He guided her into it. His mouth on hers stifled any screams, although I doubt she would have risked screaming. Despite her continued struggles, he lowered her effortlessly down into the hay on the floor.

I didn't feel much affection for Ingrid just then, not with everything that was buzzing around in my head, but she was my sister and I couldn't very well stand out here doing nothing while she was raped. I left the crack in the wall and walked with long, rapid strides around the corner of the barn, to the door. It was partially open where Kenny had neglected to close it after them. I jerked it the rest of the way open and stepped over the sill. Thus far, I had made almost no sound, and whatever noises I might have caused, they hadn't heard. They weren't listening for prowlers just then—and if Ingrid were being raped, she had progressed to being a highly willing victim.

From inside the door, I could see and hear them clearly. Realizing that they could see me too if they but looked, I instinctively stepped aside into the shadows. I was sorry at once that I had, instead of going back outside. They moved on the hay, Ingrid's face turned toward the door, and I was trapped. I couldn't leave without being seen. Ingrid was a long way from wanting her honor defended. Like it or not, there was nothing I could do but stand there and wait until he had finished fucking her.

It was an ordeal that I prayed would end quickly. He looked so much like Kenny that it was painful. Even now, doing this, he moved like Kenny. One part of me was sick at having to be a witness to this, but the other part of me was aroused by the sight of his lean hips rising and falling over her. His jeans were pulled down and his short coat rose and fell with his thrusts, baring his ass, then covering it, and baring it again. I remembered that time with Kenny, the real Kenny, and I almost believed that I had dreamed Ingrid's remark, and that this had to be Kenny after all.

I tried to tell myself that this wasn't Ingrid beneath him, her face contorted with excitement and pleasure, her limbs clinging to him. At least it wasn't the Ingrid I had known. Yet I had a strange realization that for the first time I was seeing the real Ingrid, and that it was the other one who had been unreal.

She thrashed and groaned and her hands clawed at his shoulders. "Doug, Doug," she moaned. It wasn't until later that the name registered in my stunned mind.

It was mercifully brief. Like an animal, he drove hard and fast to the end. Their muffled cries disturbed the stillness of the barn. At the other end of the building, one of the horses stirred restlessly, troubled by the sounds.

When he had come, he stood quickly, as though he no longer wanted to touch her. He turned his back on her as he stuffed himself into his jeans. I had a glimpse of his flat belly, a cloud of black hair, and his cock, growing limp now and gleaming wetly.

"Good night," he told her coldly, without even looking back at her.

She had raised herself on one elbow, but her skirt was still thrown upward, leaving her brazenly exposed, if he had cared to look.

"You were right, Doug," she said. "I did want that. Why shouldn't we…?"

He did look back then, whirling around swiftly, but it wasn't desire that moved him. "It wasn't you," he said, his voice like the crack of a whip. She stared at him stupidly, not comprehending.

121

"It wasn't you I fucked, Ingrid," he said. With that he turned on his heels and walked away. He passed within a few feet of me, without seeing me, and left the barn. I heard snow crunching beneath his feet as he walked swiftly toward the house.

I had crouched as far back in the shadows as possible. I would have given anything to do as Kenny had done and return to the house. I wanted to be done with this entire business, but Ingrid was still here. She stared after him for a long time. Then, with what sounded like a sob, she threw her hands over her face. I could see her shoulders shaking as she cried silently.

I had no idea how long she might remain here, and the desire to escape from this place was raging within me. There was a chance, a slim one, that I could reach the door without being noticed. Cursing myself for being foolish, I decided anyway to chance it.

Her face was still in her hands. I moved out of my hiding place, into the patch of moonlight that spilled through the door. I was watching her, and not my feet. That was a mistake. My foot hit a loose stone and sent it clattering across the hard floor. I jumped and turned toward her.

She couldn't help seeing me, framed as I was in the doorway.

CHAPTER FOURTEEN

"Mar."

She looked as much puzzled as surprised to see me. I realized that, in turning about as I had, I had made it impossible for her to know whether I had just come into the barn, or was going out. It must have been pride that swayed her toward the first possibility.

"I didn't hear you come in," she said. As she said it, she scrambled to her feet, trying to put her clothes back into some kind of order. I couldn't think of what to say. There was too much in my head for me to think clearly.

She fidgeted under my staring. She was tired, and in the pale light she looked haggard and much older than she really was.

"I couldn't sleep," she offered lamely. I saw the glance she threw past me toward the door. She was wondering if I had encountered Kenny. Her resources began to return to her finally and she tried to stage a recovery. "What are you doing here?"

"I don't know," I answered. That was the truth, at least. I didn't know anymore just what it was I was doing here.

"Oh." She tried to stare me down, but my face was in shadows, and even if it hadn't been, I doubt that she could have read it very well. She sighed wearily and pushed a strand of hair back from her face. "I'm tired. I'm going in."

I still stood between her and the doorway. She stepped toward me and then stopped when I didn't move out of her way.

"What about him?" I asked.

"Kenny?"

"Doug," I corrected her.

She didn't show any surprise. By then, she must have realized that I had been here for a while. I expected her to be shocked, or angry, but she didn't even flinch.

"So, you know," she said, matter-of-factly. "I thought you did."

"Not all of it," I said. As we talked, my mind was beginning to work again, and at the same time some of my anger was returning, but most of all, I wanted to understand, and I still couldn't. "Not nearly all. Who is he, Ingrid? What is this all about? What in God's name is he doing here?"

She rubbed her arms with her hands. I remembered that she had been in the barn for hours already, and despite the heaters there was a chill in the air that came through the cracks in the walls

"You can't be that stupid, Mar," she said, beginning to pace the open area in front of the stalls. "You know what he's doing here."

She was right, of course. Even I couldn't be that stupid. "Where did you find him?" I asked instead.

"Luck, sheer luck," she said, spinning around to face me again. I would have expected some remorse, some anxiety—she had been caught out in her scheme—but her face, as she moved closer to me again, was excited and eager. "It was straight from heaven, Mar. I met him in Indianapolis."

She spoke breathlessly and so rapidly that her words ran together. "I thought he was Kenny. Would you have believed two men could look so much alike? I didn't, until I had talked to him, and watched him, and seen how different they were in other ways. At first, I thought it was just funny, one of those freak things that happen. Then, when I had thought about it, I realized what he could mean. To us."

"To us?"

"Don't you see, Mar?" The more she talked, the more excited she was becoming. It may have been simply that she was trying to sell me on the idea and was using all of her enthusiasm to do so. Or perhaps Ingrid was simply in love with her own cleverness. I didn't know which, but, just now, watching her and listening to her breathless explanation, I thought of the little girl who had practiced her dancing for us, or lived for months fancying herself a great actress. "It was the answer to everything, this whole rotten business here."

I wasn't being hard to get along with. I really was having trouble following her reasoning. "What business? I thought everything was going along pretty well."

"Oh, hell," she snapped, exasperated. "What do you think all this is about, anyway? The farm, the Baker estate. Can't you see? Kenny was gone, he had been gone for five years. It was obvious he wasn't interested in any of it, or he'd have been back before this. Mrs. Baker is practically dead right now. She isn't going to be around to enjoy any of this. And who was going to get it all? The church! But they didn't deserve it, Mar, they hadn't done anything to earn it."

She was breathing hard, caught up in the excitement of her efforts. "But we did, you and Olsen and I. We had spent years building this place up, working to make something out of it—and all for the church's benefit? Do you know what reward we were going to get for all those years of work? I saw her will. I found it in her desk one day when she was out cold. Olsen was going to inherit a lousy thousand dollars, that's what. Nothing for either of us."

I could have pointed out that we had been rewarded generously during all those years: a good home, good pay, respect, even affection, but none of that seemed to have had any value to Ingrid, and I doubted that it would now.

"And then along comes Doug," she said, her voice and face triumphant. "He looked like Kenny, he acted like him in many ways—and he was smart, smart enough to learn the rest. He's even learned to do a good imitation of Kenny's handwriting. If he could come here, and pose as Kenny, convince her that he was her son, she would change her mind again, I was sure of it. Then—this is the point—then I could marry him, and we'd end up with the farm and everything. And it worked, Mar, it worked. She isn't going to change her

125

will, I'm sure of it, and in a few weeks, he and I will be married."

"And all you have to do is arrange for Mrs. Baker to die," I added coldly.

That took the funny smile off her face. "She's old, Mar," she said. "She won't live much longer. I can wait for that."

She saw finally that I didn't share her excitement, and that realization had a calming effect on her. She was back to watching me like a prizefighter, her manner suddenly wary.

"What are you going to do?" she asked after a pause.

"I don't know," I admitted honestly. All of a sudden, I was tired now, tried of this night, tired of the entire business.

"Then do nothing," she begged me, in a wheedling tone. She came to me, grabbing one of my hands in hers. Her skin might have been carved from ice, it was so cold. "That's all we need from you, your silence, and a little time. A few months, weeks maybe, and it will be ours. We'll never have to work again, or worry about the future. Think of Olsen, if nothing else. She's getting old herself, and what's in store for her—a thousand dollars, or the kind of money to keep her in comfort for the rest of her life?"

I pulled my hand from hers and turned away from her, starting toward the door. "I don't know," I said. "I'll have to think."

At the door, something crossed my mind, and I paused to look back at her. She was still standing where I had left her.

"There's just one thing that puzzles me," I said. "What about Kenny?"

"Kenny?"

"The real Kenny. What if he had come back?"

She struggled with that one for a moment, as if she had never thought of that possibility, but I did not believe that. "Why...why, we'd have had to...to do something. But he didn't."

"No, he didn't." I wondered what she had actually planned on doing if he had shown up.

126

"You'd better get to bed," I told her, going out the door. "It's almost morning."

The house was still again when I went in. Kenny was in bed by this time, and probably sound asleep, if I knew him.

I frowned as I remembered that I didn't know him, not at all, that he wasn't Kenny, that he was someone named Douglas Allen.

KENNY'S BACK, BY VICTOR J. BANIS

CHAPTER FIFTEEN

I awoke in the morning later than usual and with a dull throbbing in my head, which might have been from lack of sleep, or from the bad dreams that had plagued the brief sleep I had gotten.

The group at breakfast in the kitchen was anything but cheerful. Olsen was in poor spirits because her work had been delayed. "I've never seen anything like it," she grumbled, giving the eggs a hard time of it. "You'd think no one in this house went to bed at night, hard as it is to drag themselves out of it in the morning."

Ingrid was up by this time, and she looked even worse than I felt. I doubted that she had slept much either, or well, although she had come inside right after me the night before. She had a lot to think about just now. There was Kenny—I still thought of him as Kenny and not as Doug. It was obvious from what I had seen the night before that he wasn't taking very well to her manipulations. From what I had witnessed, she hadn't been too displeased with his revolt, up to the point when he had thrown that last insult at her.

At this stage in the game, however, Ingrid could not afford to fall back on pride. If she was going to succeed in her plans, she had no choice but to continue the masquerade of affection between herself and Kenny. Certainly she would have to go ahead with the plans for marriage. She couldn't even afford a day or so of coolness, which otherwise could have been explained away as a lovers' quarrel, because she had to tell him about me. He would have to be warned, as soon as possible, that I was on to them and knew about the entire business. She took care of that at the first opportunity.

When breakfast was over, Kenny excused himself and left the kitchen. Ingrid fidgeted for a minute before finding an excuse to go after him.

Since the scene with Ingrid in the barn, I had had time to do some thinking of my own—none of it very pleasant, but out of it all, one additional realization had taken shape. If Kenny, the real one, had returned, Ingrid would have done something, would have somehow removed him from the picture. I was sure she would not allow anything to stand in her way, and I didn't even want to think how far she would go to gain her objectives. Now, in a sense, I was in her way.

"Pete says you were outside last night looking around," Olsen interrupted my thoughts as she began clearing away the dishes.

"I thought I heard something," I said, not liking the necessity of lying to her. "I went out to check, and I didn't want Pete mistaking me for a prowler and taking a shot at me."

"Between his eyesight and that liquor of his, it's a wonder he hasn't shot down my clothesline," she said.

I had started for the door when she spoke again. "You know," she said thoughtfully, talking to the sink more than to me, "There's something bothering me about those two."

"Who?" I was stalling. I knew she wasn't talking about Pete, or about her clothesline.

"Kenny and Ingrid, and this new romance of theirs. Does it seem to you as if something's, oh, I don't know, not right?"

"They've probably had a spat about something," I said. "That happens, I understand." I tried again for the door, but she turned from the sink to face me directly, and I had no choice but to stop again.

"No, not that," she said. "It's the whole thing. Ingrid's all right. She was always crazy about Kenny, and I think she's in love with him all right. But—don't ever say I

130

mentioned this—but I somehow don't feel right about their getting married. Kenny's changed a lot, Mar, and Lord knows he was always a wild one, for all that I loved him like a son. I don't know if he even cares about her the way a man cares for the woman he marries."

You, too, I thought, *you've seen it, too, Olsen*, all this business going on below the surface. "He's proposed to her, hasn't he?" I answered aloud.

"Yes," she admitted reluctantly. After a breath, she added, "I suppose he has."

I made my escape then, but I was even more worried than before. I didn't like the knowledge that Olsen was beginning to worry and maybe even do some wondering of her own.

What if she were to become suspicious, I asked myself? For all I knew, maybe she was already. If she ever learned the truth, or even a part of it, no one would be foolish enough to gamble on her silence. Olsen was too honest for anyone to think that she might stand by and see some wrong committed. In that sense, she'd be even more of a threat than I was. She was a woman and getting on in years. If Ingrid and the phony Kenny meant to remove any obstacles to their plans, Olsen would be easily removed.

The situation was rapidly becoming uglier and uglier. I knew that I would have to do something: but what, and how?

* * * * * * *

Kenny made his move that same day. I had finished my work and, being anything but good company, had gone up to my own room. I was lying on my bed, smoking a cigarette, when he knocked at the door and came in. I didn't bother getting up. I didn't' feel much respect or friendliness toward him. Even if there was nothing else to charge him with, he had cheated me, in pretending to be someone I cared for, and by trying to fill that place in my affections.

"Ingrid said you talked to her," he said. He was direct, I gave him credit for that at least. No beating about the

131

bush now, none of the vague comments he tried with me before.

"I did," I said.

He paused. Looking up at him, I thought he looked sorry. He had reason to be, of course. I didn't imagine he was too happy at having me know.

"There's a lot you don't know about," he began again.

"I know enough, and I don't want to hear the rest."

He thought about that for a minute. "You could make things a lot easier, Mar...."

"Not me," I interrupted him. I looked up at him, speaking angrily. "No, I'm not going to help you. I don't know what I am going to do, but leave me out of your dirty dealings."

He smiled, not an amused smile, but a sad, bitter one. "I can't reach you, can I?" he said softly.

"Do me a favor, don't try," I said. "And do me another favor while you're at it. This is my room, at least it is right now. Until you own it, stay out of it."

I'd hit hard. He scowled and I expected some of the anger that I knew was beneath that handsome surface. He fooled me, though. He kept it under control, although I could see it simmering in his eyes. He didn't say anything. He stared at me for a minute, his black eyes flashing, and then he left, letting the door slam hard behind him.

He accomplished more than he had intended with his visit. He had given me a chance to realize how much I hated him for what he was doing. And he had given me the resolve that I lacked before. I knew now that I was going to upset their cart—and I knew how it could be done.

If I was going to unmask Kenny, hopefully without bringing Ingrid into it at all, I would have to outside the house—if necessary, to the local sheriff.

As things stood now, though, I'd only be going to him with a lot of crazy ideas. For all that I knew, I had no proof of anything. It would be my word against Kenny's and Ingrid's, and with a lot of ugliness to follow. If it came to a battle of wits, I was the first to admit I'd be no match for the two of them. Especially since everyone else, even Kenny's mother, had accepted him as the real thing.

There was proof, though, one person who might be made to see the truth, if he hadn't already seen it, and who might be persuaded to take a stand with me. I didn't like it, but I had no choice. If there was anyone who by now was likely to have guessed that Kenny was not genuine, it was Dexter. No matter how clever the handsome young man who had just left my room might be, I was sure there were some things he couldn't successfully fake. Only two of us would have been able to judge those things, and of the two of us, only Holloman had had experience with both Kenny and his double.

* * * * * * *

I was probably the last person that Holloman expected to have call on him. As I pulled up the drive and parked in front of his house, I saw a curtain pulled aside from one of the windows, and I knew that my arrival had been noticed.

Even so, there was a long silence after I rang the bell, and I half suspected that he wasn't going to answer the door. He had good reason for being hesitant, I suppose. The last time I had come to call on him, he had been carrying on with Kenny, and I had ended by knocking him cold. Now, five years later, he was back to his old tricks, with someone who was supposed to be Kenny. He might very well think I had come to deliver the same comment on his behavior.

He did finally open the door, however, looking puzzled and not too enthusiastic to see me, although he managed a neighborly greeting.

"I'd like to talk to you," I said when it became apparent that he was waiting for some explanation of my visit. "Can I come in?"

"Of course." He remained puzzled, but with only a slight hesitation, he stepped back and let me into the house. I followed him into the big front room. The house didn't seem to have changed much from what I remembered of it in the past.

"Drink?" he asked. When I declined, he stepped to a makeshift bar to refill the glass in his own hand. I waited in silence, looking him over at the same time.

"You've come about Kenny, I suppose," he said finally, when he had fixed his drink and turned his attention back to me.

I was glad to get right to the point. "We may as well save some time. I know he's been coming over here at night, and it isn't hard to guess why."

He considered his words before reply. Probably he was deciding how angry I might be, and what risks there were for him. "I could say, of course, that it's none of your concern, not any longer," he said. "He's of age, not a child. You're neither a relative nor a guardian."

"True enough," I said. I looked around for a chair. "Mind if I sit down," and sat without being asked. He sat too. He was still looking wary, waiting for some explanation of my visit.

"Maybe it will make things easier for you," I began again, "If I say I don't much care what you do or don't do with Kenny."

He looked relieved at that, but even more puzzled. "I see," he answered simply, and waited for me to go on.

"Except," I added, "There are things I want to know, things only you can tell me."

"Such as?"

"What it's like with him—then, and now."

He relaxed a little more, and his smile became a smirk. I could easily imagine the thoughts crossing his mind. I gave serious consideration to changing my mind about punching him again.

"Perhaps you should go to him for that," he suggested.

"No, thanks. It isn't details that I'm after," I told him. "I don't need blow by blow descriptions." I decided to take the plunge. "What I want to know is whether it's different."

That got past the smirk. There was a quick reaction, a frown that crossed his face, a narrowing of the eyes. "What do you mean, different?" he asked in a low voice.

134

"Just that. You knew him before. Before he went away. And he's been over here since he came back. You've had chances to look at him differently from anyone else. How much has Kenny changed?"

He thought about that before he answered, and when he did, he spoke slowly and deliberately. "He's changed, of course. Everyone does, over that period of time. But I don't see...."

"Enough," I leaned forward in my chair, taking a deep breath, "Enough to make you think he might not be Kenny?"

He met my gaze evenly. A veil had dropped over his face, and there was neither amusement nor surprise showing now. "No," he said finally.

I swallowed my disappointment, pausing to chew at one knuckle of my hand. "What if I told you he wasn't Kenny," I tried again. I had taken it too fast, sprung it on him too abruptly, I could see that belatedly, but now that I was in the water, I couldn't do anything but swim. "Think about that for a moment," I went on quickly. "Is there anything you have seen or done, that comes back to you? Isn't it even possible, no matter how crazy, that he could be someone else?"

All I needed from him was a faint suspicion, something I could work on and develop. If he would only admit the possibility, I had something to go after.

"And if he weren't Kenny?" he asked. "What then?"

The question startled me, and for a moment I was at a loss. "Why, we'd have to expose him as an impostor," I said.

Dexter stood up, turning his back on me to stare out the window at the fields separating his house from ours. "I can't help you, I'm afraid," he said after a long silence.

I had struck out again, and this time there was an air of finality in his denial. "Then you think he really is Kenny," I said, "That I am imagining the rest?"

"I mean simply that I can't help you," he said.

"Can't, or won't?" I was thinking of what helping me would mean to him: the scandal and the dredging up of the past. I thought that it was this that prompted his answer, but when he turned, I saw that he was smiling faintly, and I knew there was something more, something I could not yet fathom.

"Won't," he answered simply.

There didn't seem to be anything I could say. I sat and stared stupidly at him, puzzled by that smile—again, a smirk, really—and felt defeated.

Dexter moved finally, going to the desk in one corner, and removed something from one of its drawers to bring it to me. At first, I didn't understand. Then comprehension began to filter into my mind. I recognized the scarf, hand painted in Italy.

"Your sister left this here accidentally," he said in a voice that was soft but unpleasant. "I wonder if you would be good enough to return it to her."

It was his moment of triumph, and he was beaming now, unquestionably pleased by my shock. Not even the anger rising up within me, which must have shown on my face, frightened away that smile of his. I ran a finger over the scarf. She had dropped it, apparently, just this morning. I remembered that she had taken the car to drive into town, and she had been wearing the scarf at her neck then.

How many other trips to town, I wondered, had brought her in this direction? She hadn't wasted any time getting to him with the news about me, that was obvious. Probably she had guessed what I would try, and as usual, she had been faster than I was. I was beaten, before I had even really gotten a start, and Holloman was enjoying my defeat immensely.

There wasn't any point in my staying. I had my answer. Holloman wasn't going to help me. That was plain. He was my proof, all right. He knew beyond any shadow of a doubt that Kenny was an impostor. What I had not counted on was that he might be involved in the scheme as well. And for all the proof that I had uncovered, it wasn't worth a damn to me. He could smirk and flaunt the scarf before me, and there was nothing I could do.

I stood wordlessly and started toward the door. Holloman wasn't finished savoring his victory, though.

"I've enjoyed our little visit," he called after me.

I paused and turned back. For a moment I was close to giving him a physical demonstration of my feelings on the matter. It must have showed, because his smile faded and his face went pale, and he took a step backward. That wasn't going to get me anywhere, though. I left him, finding my own way out, and slammed the door after myself.

That was that, I told myself as I drove back to the farm. I had counted on Holloman as the confirming evidence that I needed for my story, only to find out that he was on their team, or at least, on Ingrid's.

* * * * * * *

I knew something was up as soon as I drove the Jeep up the drive into the barnyard. There was a strange car there. I was halfway across the yard before I recognized Dr. Keith's old Chevy. When I did, I began suddenly to run.

Ingrid had heard the Jeep coming up the drive. She opened the door as I bounded up the front steps. I don't know what I expected to see in her face—grief, shock, triumph—but there was nothing. Her voice, as she told me, was calm and even, as though she might be speaking of the weather.

"Mrs. Baker's dead," was all she said.

KENNY'S BACK, BY VICTOR J. BANIS

CHAPTER SIXTEEN

Olsen felt the death keenly. In their own way the two women had been friends as well as employer and employee. Olsen's answer to her grief was the same as she used for most troubles: she worked harder than ever.

"It's good to keep busy," she answered when I suggested she ought to take it easy, and I didn't argue the matter. In any case, I knew she could take it and in all truthfulness, I didn't much worry over it.

I would have expected Ingrid to feel a real sense of triumph. The prize she had worked for was practically in her hands.

The truth was, though, that she seemed to be almost dazed by Mrs. Baker's death. At first, this mystified me, but then I began to understand the probable reason for it. She had plotted and worked and had come close to success, but in actual fact, there was still a wide gulf between her and the end of her journey. The prize she had fought for was in Kenny's hands, not hers, and until they were married, she had accomplished nothing. There was a proposal, of course, that she had managed to make him commit himself to, but she certainly knew that her partner in her efforts had a mind of his own, and could be hard to deal with.

No doubt she had counted on being Mrs. Baker before the other woman with that name passed away. As it had turned out, propriety would force a delay. Kenny could hardly marry right away, even if he were willing. There would have to be a respectable mourning period, and during that time he would have control of the estate she had expected. It must have given her some real cause for worry.

It was harder still to understand the fake Kenny's reaction to the death. Like Ingrid, he too seemed to be in a daze, but in his case, I couldn't apply the same explanation. It looked as though he came out on top of the heap, but whatever pleasure it gave him was well concealed.

At the same time, I would have expected a man as clever as he obviously was to put on a better show of grief. He looked stunned, but I saw not a single sign of tears or mourning. When he emerged from Mrs. Baker's room on the afternoon of her death, there was an ashen color to his face, but his eyes were dry and his manner guarded and rigidly controlled. He had little to say to anyone, and, in fact, avoided us all as much as possible, keeping to his room or going out of the house to wander around alone.

"He must be taking it terribly hard," Olsen said, watching him through the kitchen window. For myself, I thought he was either a far better actor than I had thought before, or a far worse one. I couldn't decide which.

I myself felt the kind of sadness one always feels when exposed to death. I had respected the woman whose life had ended, and felt almost a family type affection for her. At the same time, though, we had not been truly close. In all our dealings we had been business associates first, friends second. I suppose if there had been someone to feel sorry for among the living, my grief might have been greater. There was Olsen, and of course there were other friends, but knowing as I did that Kenny was not really her son, I could scarcely have any sympathy for him.

Somewhere there was a real Kenny, and the real sadness I felt was actually for him. I thought of him someplace distant, not even knowing what had happened, never having now the chance to reconcile himself to her, as she believed he had. I would have liked to search through her effects, with the hope that I might find some trace of him, and could let him know, but I had no claim to them and no way of doing so. I didn't even know where such a clue might be. Chances were that, if it had existed at all, it existed in the mind of the dead woman, and the secret had gone with her.

I didn't like to face some of the thoughts that went through my mind during the first several hours after the death. I thought of Ingrid and the false Kenny, and I thought of the threat I had posed to their plot. It was not entirely impossible that they had taken a course of action more direct than any I had expected of them. I questioned Olsen about the death, to such a length that she was puzzled by my curiosity, and I had to shelve my questions. But Olsen was no fool, and obviously she had no suspicions, and there was not a trace of evidence to suggest that the death was anything but the natural one it seemed.

Ingrid had been with Olsen most of the afternoon, except when she had gone into town. I knew full well where that trip had taken her. As for Kenny, he had been outside somewhere. The important fact was that Mrs. Baker had spent the day alone or with Olsen nearby. Later, Olsen told me that Mrs. Baker had been feeling poorly for days, and that her mind had even seemed to wander.

"She asked for Kenny," Olsen explained sadly, "And when I said I'd call him, she said something about wishing he'd return."

I wondered if, after all, Mrs. Baker hadn't known the truth all along and, for some reason known only to herself, kept it a secret. It was a question, however, which would remain forever unanswered.

"I heard a crash," Olsen described the death. "I knew right away what it was. She must have gotten out of bed for some reason, heaven only knows what, or why she didn't ring for me. When I went in, she was on the floor. She'd knocked over the little table by her bed when she fell, and she must have died at once.

Later, when I had thought of Ingrid's new dilemma, I decided that there hadn't been anything questionable about the death. Mrs. Baker had been near death for a long time. She had finally and simply done what had been inevitable.

* * * * * * *

The greatest and most violent mourning was done by someone whom Mrs. Baker had always especially loved: Nature.

From the first evening, the weather went crazy. It snowed, not the quiet, wistful snows we'd had already this season, but a violent fury that shook the house and left us half buried in white drifts. It cleared the next day, long enough for the highway workmen to get a good start on cleaning the roads, and then it started again. By the morning of the funeral, Hanover and the surrounding countryside was firmly in the grips of a real winter storm.

The weather made its influence felt on the funeral, of course. There was a respectable crowd at the funeral home for the services, but very few tried to make the drive to the cemetery, over a road that was only half cleared and rapidly shutting down again. The few of us who did go—those of us from the farmhouse and one or two others—stood in bitter cold in a patch of frozen ground from which the snow had been cleared, and tried to ignore our discomfort long enough to concentrate on the brief words of the minister.

I found myself throughout the entire ceremony concentrating the greatest part of my attention on the man posing as the son of the deceased. He seemed to have lost all of his brazen self-confidence and, even knowing what I did of him, it was hard to think of him as anything but a man much younger than his actual years who for a brief period had sealed himself off from us in a world of his own.

He wore a suit that had been Kenny's and had spent five years in a closet in Kenny's room. It was too small for him and with his wrists and ankles sticking out from it he looked awkward and lanky, like he had grown up too fast. At the funeral and at the cemetery, he remained to himself, and the mask that concealed whatever he was feeling never slipped from its place. He moved mechanically and went through all the motions of mourning as though acting a part in a bad play.

Before we even left the cemetery the snow had started up again, a bad wind blowing it in our faces in thick clouds. People were talking about being snowed in, and there were even some folks, living off the main highways, who were already confined to their homes by the thick drifts of snow. I didn't need Olsen's aching joints to tell me that we were in for the kind of nasty storm that every several years managed to paralyze the countryside, sometimes for days.

Kenny came and went from the funeral by himself, in the Jeep. I drove Olsen and Ingrid and Pete in the Buick. It was warmer than the drafty Jeep, but by the time we had slipped and skidded home over roads it was hard to locate, let alone drive, I envied Kenny the safety of the Jeep's better handling, cold drafts or not.

He was home before us. The Jeep was already snug inside the barn by the time I pulled the sedan in out of the blinding snow. I looked after the animals briefly and ran, none too steadily, to the house.

"Was Kenny in the barn?" Olsen asked me as I burst into the kitchen.

"Didn't see him," I answered, busily shaking the snow from my clothes and shedding the heavy coat I had worn. "Isn't he here?"

"No, he's nowhere in the house." She looked in the direction of the kitchen window, at the storm gathering force outside. "You don't suppose...?" She left the suggestion unfinished.

"He'd have no reason to be out in that," I assured her, but the fact was, he obviously must have gone out in it. I checked for myself, going from room to room through the house, but Kenny was not there. While I tried to act calm, and kept assuring Olsen there was nothing to worry about, I was beginning to worry myself. It was only mid-afternoon, but already as dark as twilight outside and anything but a good place for a man to be.

There was one possibility that occurred to me, and when I had a moment alone with Ingrid, I told her to call Holloman. She gave me a startled look, but by this time she was growing worried herself for her own reasons. She did as I suggested, and came back to the kitchen, and as soon as Olsen had looked away from us, Ingrid gave me an anxious shake of her head.

We passed the afternoon in tense waiting. Night came, and beyond the tufts of snow that slapped against the window there was blackness as solid as coal. We were all really alarmed by now. More than one man had found this sort of weather to be stronger than he was, and the blackness of night made it vastly more dangerous.

"Thank God it's Kenny," Olsen said at one point, starting dispiritedly to prepare supper. "Someone who didn't know this area, or this kind of weather, wouldn't have a chance out there."

I echoed the alarm on Ingrid's face. With all the waiting and worrying, neither of us had thought of that before. It wasn't Kenny, of course, who was out in the storm. It was someone who, for all we knew, didn't know the first thing about this kind of weather—and less about the area. I knew then what I had to do.

"Mar!" Olsen gave me a startled look as I took my coat down from the hook on which it was hanging.

"I've got to look for him," I said evenly. "If he's still out in this, he's either crazy or he can't make it back."

"But where?" Ingrid asked, conflicting emotions crossing her face. "How will you know where to look?"

I thought for a moment, my forehead wrinkled with worry. It came to me then, one possible answer. I'll never know what brought it to my mind. Of all the places I might have looked, I would later realize that this was the most unlikely.

At the moment, it was all I could think of.

CHAPTER SEVENTEEN

If I had stopped for a minute to think, I'd have known that my hunch was a crazy one, that it couldn't be possible. But I didn't think about it, I acted upon it, following some instinctive hunch that, as I began to prepare to face the storm, gelled in my mind into something very like a certainty.

I took an extra coat and blankets, and when I came back into the kitchen, Olsen had filled a large thermos with hot soup.

"He may be frozen by now," she said, putting it in my hands. "You'll both need this before you get back."

"If we don't get back right away, don't worry," I said at the door. "We may have to sit out the storm."

I saw from her face that she knew better. Every hour that I was gone would only lessen the possibility of returning safely. But she said nothing. She had brought her Bible to the kitchen, and she held it tightly in both her hands. I knew that she would spend the time praying for me, for both of us. I was grateful. We would need all the prayers we could get.

For a moment I was even tempted to interpret Ingrid's obvious anxiety as sisterly affection, but I reminded myself that she had other reasons for being worried. With a final glance at the two of them, I went out.

It was like moving through a swirling fog of white flakes. The wind pushed me back, trying to deny me the right to be out with it, but I fought my way across the yard to the

145

barn. Pete was there, looking after the animals and battening things down. Even with the heaters in the barn, the place was like an icebox. I saw that he had put blankets across Jezebel and Ladyship. I didn't stop to talk to him, knowing that he would take good care of everything here.

He stopped in his work when he saw me climbing into the Jeep. "You're crazy," he yelled over the coughing of the engine. "You'll just run into the pear tree with that thing. You can't see your hand in front of your face out there."

"Kenny's missing," I yelled back, giving the engine a chance to warm up.

Pete walked over to the Jeep. "Wait'll I get my things, I'll go too," he said without any hesitation.

I shook my head and shifted gears. "You look after things here."

He might have argued, but at that moment the lights in the barn dimmed, came bright again, and went out. I looked over my shoulder, but there was no light showing from the house. A line had gone down someplace nearby.

"Olsen and Ingrid are alone in the house," I said. "You'd better get up there and keep them quiet. They'll need you there, if..." I didn't finish the sentence, but he knew I was talking about the fact that I might not make it back. He didn't argue further, but stepped back from the Jeep with a nod of his head.

By the time I had backed into the barnyard and turned around, I was beginning to think he was right about taking the Jeep out. It was impossible to see more than a few inches ahead. Shadows loomed out of the whiteness and I found myself skidding around trees that I would have sworn should have been somewhere else. I nearly took a corner of Pete's shack with me, and I hated to think what Olsen was going to say about the damage to her rose bushes. When I hit the fence instead of passing through the gate, I decided the Jeep was useless.

"I'd just have to leave it in the woods anyway," I consoled myself, jumping down into snow that was drifted hip high in places. I made a makeshift pack out of the blankets and things, pulled my collar high and tied my bandana over my face, and started out on foot.

It was slow walking, with the weight dragging at my feet and the snow and wind together trying to hold me back. I fell twice, stumbling over a log and over a broken fence that was buried in a drift. It seemed like I had walked half way around the world by the time I reached the edge of the woods. My hands and feet were quickly growing numb even through their protective coverings, and it was more a matter of falling over the fence there than climbing it.

It was easier in the woods, though. The thick old trees offered some break in the wind, and the snow was less deep here. I found a stray dog in one of the traps Pete had set earlier. He was dead by now, frozen into a solid form. Later, I'd have to come back and bury him, but for the present I could do nothing but run a gloved hand sadly down his back and leave him where he was.

Instinct alone must have guided me, as it would have been impossible to find a path or follow any sort of trail. Every tree looked alike, and it was a miracle that I wasn't making my way around in a big circle.

Somehow, though, I went right, or mostly so. I recognized a briar patch where Kenny, Ingrid and I had once found a nest of baby rabbits whose mother had been some hunter's catch. I remembered how we had tried to raise them, feeding them with eyedroppers. When they died, we had a big funeral right here beside the patch, with Kenny solemnly reading from Olsen's Bible. I don't suppose the rabbits cared much for the Ten Commandments, but it had been an impressive ceremony and all three of us had been moved to tears.

"Thou shalt not steal....Thou shalt not covet....Thou shalt not...." The words ran together in my memory, and I shook my head, afraid I was getting delirious, and pushed on.

The woods were a sea of memories, though. Every tree brought Kenny back to me, every hill and knoll reminded me of those past years. We had hunted mushrooms and berries here, hiked and played and fought. The memories were painful, but they were also the spark that kept me moving and prevented me thinking of how cold I was, or how tired I was becoming.

I realized belatedly that I had gone wrong after all. I had forgotten Black Creek stood between me and my destination. Downstream it was shallower and not too hard to cross even if it wasn't frozen, but I had come up to it at the deep part. Guided by those instincts, I had taken the path that Kenny and I had so often taken when we were younger, and I had come out at the swimming hole. There was ice on the surface, but Black Creek was fast moving, and I wasn't sure it was yet frozen solid enough to walk on.

I was in the open here, and back to the full blast of the wind. It was a half mile down to the shallows, and a half mile back up the other side, fighting the wind and snow all the way.

"If it breaks, Mar," I told myself aloud, putting one foot cautiously on the ice, "You'll have ice cubes for balls."

I moved slowly, pausing each time the ice creaked beneath me. I fell once and in that second as I hit the ice, my heart stopped beating. If I once went through, there was little chance of ever escaping from the frigid water. The ice held, though, and I half walked, half crawled the rest of the way. I was even glad, as I finished the tedious crossing, to be back in the drifts of snow.

On the other side the ground shot upward in a bluff. Beyond that, on the hillside leading down, was the cave. I hadn't been there in years, but I could picture it as clearly as in a photograph. It had been our place, Kenny's and mine— our secret hideout, our retreat from the common world, and the place where we had first started to play around.

It was the only place, too, where a man would last for long on a night like this. If he wasn't here, there wasn't any chance of ever finding him until the storm had ended. If he wasn't in the cave, protected from the wind and the snow and the cold, there wasn't going to be much of a hurry about looking for him, either.

I almost missed it. It was sheltered by an overhang, so that you couldn't see the opening until you were right there at it. I passed the knoll and then realized my mistake and circled back to it.

"Kenny!" I shouted as I clambered toward the small opening, but the wind caught my shout and carried it upward and away in a rush.

The opening had seemed bigger in the past. I had always had to stoop, but now I managed to scrape my back, and earned myself a good bump on the head before I got through the small passageway to the place where the cave widened out and even a tall man could stand with no trouble.

I must have scared him all but witless, my sudden appearance, snow covering me from head to foot. I stumbled to a standing position and almost toppled back down into the fire he had built. It was warm and musty smelling in there, and as quiet as if there had never been a storm raging outside.

"Mar?" He jumped to his feet and darted around the fire to support me. I had come to rescue him, and here he was helping me back around the fire to where I could sit down on one of the big rocks.

"You damned fool," I greeted him when I had gotten my breath back. "We thought you'd be frozen stiff by now." At the moment, I didn't much appreciate that I had spent the better part of two hours tramping through snow, freezing my feet and hands into solid chunks of ice, only to find him as cozy and snug as if he were in front of the fireplace at home.

"It looks like you're the one who's frozen," he said. He was busy getting my snow-caked coat off of me. "Here, get out of some of these things and we'll get them dry."

"There's soup in the thermos," I said through clacking teeth as he removed the clumsy pack from my shoulders. I wasn't much help to him yet. My fingers were pretty useless just then. With me making the job more difficult by trying to help, Kenny managed to get my gloves and boots off. The moisture of the snow had soaked through my coat, and my shirt and pants were unpleasantly wet by this time.

"Better get out of them, too," he said, unbuttoning my shirt. "It's plenty warm in here, and they'll dry faster if they're loose."

We made a pretty silly looking pair by the time he was done. I sat naked as a jaybird with a blanket about my shoulders and between my bare ass and the rock. Kenny was still in the suit he had worn to the funeral, and not much ruffled for all the time he had been gone. He must have come straight here from the cemetery. When I asked, he told me he had.

"When the storm got worse, I figured I'd better try to sit it out," he explained, pouring some of the hot soup into the cap of the thermos. "I probably would have frozen, trying to get home dressed like this. And I knew everyone would be worried, but I never thought...."

He stopped, his hand frozen in the act of handing me the soup, his eyes wide with wonder, his mouth agape. "You came for me, Mar," he said in a small, peculiar voice. "You came here to find me—here, to our cave."

We sat like that for the longest time, staring without saying anything or moving. Then, all of a sudden, Olsen's broth was a puddle on the floor of the cave, and he was in my arms.

I forgot about the storm, about being cold and tired and hungry, forgot about everything but the lean, hard body in my arms. He left me once, to spread the other blanket on the solid ground a little further back in the cave—and to take off that suit. After that, we didn't look funny together.

I was like a wild man. I wanted to explore every inch of his flesh. I had wanted that since I had first looked from the window and seen him sauntering up the drive. This time I didn't have to be asked to put his cock in my mouth, and it didn't matter or slow me down when I choked on the unfamiliar length of it. I held his little ass in my big hands, cupping the firm cheeks in each palm, and lifted him easily from the blanket, pulling him up to me with a desperate hunger. His stomach rolled with his breathing, his hips thrust powerfully against me.

When his mouth closed over me, I thought my chest would burst open from the excitement within. I groaned aloud and reached for him, sucking him into my mouth again. We fucked like that, our faces buried in one another's thighs, our bodies rocking and shoving together. His balls slapped against my chin and I kissed them, too, and thought they were more beautiful than anything I could remember.

150

It wasn't the first cock he had sucked since we had last been together, but I didn't let myself think of where he had gotten his experience. I almost choked to death when he came, sending a hot torrent down into my throat that nearly turned my stomach inside out. He didn't have a problem, although he had a full-scale flood to contend with. He drained me completely, until I fell away from him, limp all over.

Later, when I had gotten my breath back, I fucked him from behind. He took me to the hilt, and his groans were more like sounds of pleasure than pain. He came again when I did, filling my hand with the proof of his pleasure.

After that, so suddenly that I was unprepared for it, I fell asleep, overcome with exhaustion.

* * * * * * *

When I awoke, he was gone. My first memory was of the guilt I had suffered the first time I had done these things. It flashed through my mind that he might have experienced the same reactions, and had run away. By the time I had jumped up, though, and started to struggle into my dry pants, he was back, scrambling through the entrance of the cave. He was dressed, wearing that silly looking suit that looked even worse in a cave than it had at the funeral, and over it, the other coat I had brought with me.

"It's stopped snowing," he greeted me. "Feel up to doing some fast traveling?"

I nodded, understanding in an instant what he meant. It was far closer to sunrise than sundown. By now, the people waiting at the house would be beside themselves worrying. More importantly, however, there was no telling when the snow would start up again. If we meant to make it back to the farm, we would have to go while the going was good.

I was dressed in no more than three minutes. Kenny put out the fire and collected our things. We draped the blankets around our shoulders for extra warmth, but Kenny refused to wear my gloves or hat.

There was so much that should have been said between us, questions to be asked and answered. They would have to wait, though. For now, there was the difficult hike

151

back to the farm, for which we would need all of our energy and breath. Maybe, too, there was the feeling that what had happened was something to do, not to talk about.

In any case, neither of us mentioned it, but concentrated on getting safely back. Even with the snow having stopped, it wasn't to be an easy trip. The wind was still blowing, although not quite as hard. It threw wisps of snow into our faces. We took the longer route to the shallow stretch of the creek, rather than risking another trip across the ice. The weight of both of us, I was sure, would be more than it would support.

The snow didn't start falling again until we were almost home. We found the spot where I had left the Jeep, but only a fender and the top of the windshield stuck out of a drift of snow, and we didn't even try to dig it out.

Pete had started out after us. He came toward us across the yard like a mountain of blankets and coats, waving a lantern before him. Funny as he looked, I hadn't seen too many sights in my life more welcome than that battered old face peering from beneath a torn quilt. The difficult trip to the cave, the sex there, and the hike back, were having their effects on me. I was glad for Pete's supporting arm the last few yards.

It was a brief reunion that took place in the kitchen, in the glow of kerosene lamps. Kenny and I were none too steady on our feet, and Olsen and Ingrid cried and fussed over us.

We let Olsen order us into chairs and got down a couple bowls of broth before Kenny started to fall asleep in his chair. With Pete and Olsen helping us, and Ingrid running ahead to open doors and turn down beds, we made it to our rooms.

At least, I made it to mine. In all honesty, I didn't know much after that. The last thing I remember was Olsen tugging at one of my boots, and a branch of the pear tree waving a hearty welcome to me at the window, with the dawn sky behind it.

CHAPTER EIGHTEEN

By morning, the power was on again, and the storm was over, although the evidence of its presence remained with us. From the newscasts we learned of people who had been trapped or stranded during the night, but by now snow crews were at work clearing the roads, and only the most isolated houses remained cut off.

Kenny was still in bed, but Olsen assured me he was suffering nothing worse than some frostbite and fatigue. She would have had me spend the day in bed too, but I got my way on that, and by early afternoon I was out with Pete looking over the damage that had been done around the place, which was slight, and clearing paths where needed. As a result, it was evening, close to suppertime, before I saw Kenny, although Olsen kept me informed as to how he was feeling.

He still looked tired and drawn when he came down into the kitchen where Olsen, Ingrid and I were seated. He had aged a lot in the last few days. The air of boyish mischief had left him to be replaced by a new maturity that did nothing to lessen his devilish good looks.

Ingrid jumped up from the table and went to him at once, throwing her arms around him and her head against his chest. Kenny didn't return her embrace, though. He stared at me over her shoulder the whole time, his eyes on mine. I saw him swallow hard, once. I think I did the same thing.

153

"It's all over," Ingrid said finally, stepping back to look anxiously up into his face. It wasn't all over, she must have realized that, and she was trying hard to find out just what was happening. "I know how much of a shock this has been for you, losing your mother and all. But it will be all right again, you'll see. In a short time we can be married, and...."

Kenny looked at her then for the first time, not maliciously or defiantly, but with something almost like pity in his face. I think it was that, his expression, that stopped her in mid-sentence.

"You're right, Ingrid it is all over," he said at last. "But we aren't going to be married. Not in a few months, not ever."

She was stunned and, for a moment, silent. Then she stepped back from him, her face angry, her head defiantly high. "What are you saying?" she demanded. It was the voice and the face that I remembered from that night in the barn, the other Ingrid. A look of surprise came over Olsen's face as she saw the change.

"Just that," Kenny said. "We aren't getting married. I'm leaving here, tomorrow, if the roads are clear."

"Oh, Kenny, no," Olsen cried. She reached out her hand toward him and then checked herself.

"No is right," Ingrid said sharply. "You aren't leaving here now, and you aren't backing out of our marriage. There's too much at stake. Or do you want to discuss that now, in front of them?"

"Do as you wish," he answered her simply, stepping around her to pour himself a cup of coffee.

"I'll tell them, I mean it," she almost shouted at him. "I'll tell everyone."

"Tell what?" Olsen asked, bewildered by the rapid chain of events that, to her, were inexplicable.

"That he isn't Kenny." Ingrid flung the words at his back.

"Of course he's Kenny." Olsen looked at her daughter as though she might have lost her mind.

"He's not," Ingrid said. "Mar knows it. He's Douglas Allen, from Indiana. He came here to pose as Kenny, so that

154

we could inherit the farm. It was all planned. And now he's got the farm, and he wants to run out on me, but I won't...."

"I haven't got the farm," Kenny said. He turned back to her then. "It isn't mine, Ingrid, or yours."

I don't think Ingrid was any more at a loss than I was. She looked at me with wide eyes, but I was dumbfounded too.

"But of course it is," she managed to say finally. "The will—it was left to you, the entire estate, everything."

He shook his head, and there was a suggestion of a smile on his lips. "That's not enough to make it mine, though," he said. "I haven't earned it, and I damned well don't deserve it. Oh, I talked to my mother about it, when you would leave us alone. I tried to coax her to leave it to Mar and Olsen. They're the ones who've made it what it is. But she was too much a businesswoman for that. Anyway, she had intended leaving it to the church before I came back. Isn't that what you told me?"

"Yes, but that...."

"I wish, frankly, she had changed her will. That would have prevented any of this from happening. But I can still see to it. I don't want this place. Mar and Olsen can have it. And the lawyers can work out some sort of an arrangement so that a share of the income goes to the church. That way, everyone will be happy. At least, everyone but you, and I'm sure Mar and Olsen will see you are taken care of, at least."

Ingrid was still too stunned to react to that last barb. She stared stupidly at him, trying to comprehend what he was telling her. "Then you won't have anything?" she asked finally.

"The little farm," he said. "That's why I went with you that day to look at it. I'll keep that for myself, and it will provide for my needs and wants quite well, even if I'll never be rich off of it."

For a moment Ingrid looked defeated. She didn't seem to grasp that the farm would be ours now, that she could continue to live here in comfort without fear of the future. But her schemes had never really been for my benefit, or Olsen's. She had wanted it all for herself.

She recovered, then, and her face went ugly again. "But you can't," she said, "I won't let you. I'll expose you as a fake, and the whole business will be thrown out. You'll go to jail for posing as Kenny."

All of this had been a little fast and furious for me, and I was still a little dizzy from trying to understand it all myself, but at last we had come back to solid ground, where I could be more sure of myself.

"He wasn't posing," I said. It was the first I had spoken. Ingrid turned on me as though she didn't know who I was. My only thought for her was that she looked like a trapped animal, making a last, desperate stand.

"He was. You know he was." She started to cry in anger and frustration. I felt sorry for her, and I almost wished I could tell her she was right, but I couldn't.

"I thought he was," I admitted slowly. "I thought for a long time that he, and you, were fooling all of us. But it was only you he was fooling, Ingrid. He really *is* Kenny."

I was almost glad to see that, with all the surprises everyone was flinging about, I had managed to get in one of my own. I saw Kenny's eyebrows go up and his mouth fall open.

"How did you...?" he started to ask, and then he realized the answer to his own question, and blushed.

"Don't you think I'd have known last night?" I knew what he was remembering and I was pleased to see his blush deepen, but he grinned shyly, and my heart nearly burst at the sight of it. It had been long years since he had grinned at me just that way.

Olsen only looked confusedly from one of us to the other, but Ingrid may have guessed what it was we were referring to. In any case, she realized suddenly that I was right, and that Kenny was really Kenny.

"You are," she said in astonishment, shaking her head and taking a step away from him. "My God, you really are. All the time...."

She had lost. After all her scheming and her efforts and coming, as she had seen it, so close, she had lost, and she realized it at last. She shot a look around the room that swept over the three of us with the coldness of the previous night's winds. Then, with a muffled cry, she turned and started quickly from the room.

There was a lot that Olsen didn't yet understand, maybe never would, but she was Ingrid's mother and a woman of deep compassion.

"Ingrid," she cried, starting after her daughter.

"Don't touch me!" Ingrid whirled on her with a vicious fury, spitting her words in her mother's face. "I hate you, all of you. You're fools, stupid, cloddish fools. And you," she turned her venom on Kenny, "You're the greatest fool of all. You got away, you could have been something, and you came back here, to this God-forsaken place. You didn't even come back for the money, you came back because...." She nearly said it. Her eyes darted in my direction, and I knew then that she understood about Kenny and me. Thank God, for Olsen's sake, that there was still some spark of decency left in Ingrid. She left it unsaid and ran from the room. Olsen moved to go after her.

"Let her go," I said quietly. It wasn't maliciousness. No matter if we were able to forgive her and forget, Ingrid would never do either. She would never again be able to bear any of us, or this house. I was sure of that. We had witnessed her defeat, her humiliation, and for that I knew she would never forgive us.

But of course, Olsen was a mother. She looked at me with tears in her eyes and, with a silent shake of her head, left the room after Ingrid.

We were alone together, Kenny and I. For a long moment we were both too preoccupied with all that had happened to grasp that fact. When we did, we looked at one another as though we were strangers. And, I suppose, in a sense, we were.

It was Kenny who spoke first. "You knew, last night, when we...?"

I nodded. "I think I must have known all along, on some instinctive level," I said, "I knew in my heart where I would find you last night, didn't I? And who else but you would have known to go there? But I got pretty confused at times. There were so many things that didn't make any sense, mistakes you made, things that didn't seem like Kenny. I still don't understand a lot of it."

He smiled and looked thoughtfully down at the floor. "I guess it must have been pretty mixed up from where you sat. Some of it was just honest mistakes, you know. There was a lot I had forgotten. And some of it I had to pretend, for Ingrid's benefit. There were things she hadn't told me or didn't know about."

"When you first arrived, when you saw Pete...."

"And I didn't throw my arms around him? I wanted to, God, I wanted to so badly, but she hadn't told me that Kenny always did that. I hinted about it time and time again before I came, but she didn't explain that. So I couldn't do it, you see. And there were other things she simply didn't know about, so I couldn't let on I knew about them either."

I laughed and shook my head, still a bit bewildered. "It was crazy," I said, "I kept telling myself it couldn't be, that I had to be imagining it all, but you and Ingrid—the business of the will, and the letter—I kept going in circles. How in God's name did it all start, anyway? I could understand it if you really were an impostor, at least then it would make sense to cook up a scheme like this, in the hopes of getting the money. But why did you do it? Why pretend to be who you really are?"

He fished a cigarette out of his pocket and lit it from the burner on the stove before he answered me. Just then I think I had heard more than I could digest at one setting, but I realized that he wanted to talk, he needed to get all this off his chest, and I let him go ahead.

"I'd wanted to come back since the very first, since five years ago. I wrote to you time and again...."

"I never got the letters," I interrupted him.

"I realized that later. Ingrid had told me the real Kenny was in California. It wasn't until later that I realized she could only know that from my letters to you."

I thought about that for a minute. "She used to bring the mail up to the house back then," I said, "Before Pete started taking care of it."

"I doubt if she was being malicious," he said. "She was just a kid, then, you know, and I guess a lot of what

happened was probably kept form her, so she was curious.
When she saw a letter in my handwriting, she probably
opened it without thinking. Afterward, when she realized
what she had done, I suppose she got scared and threw it
away, without daring to mention it to anyone."

"Good thing for her she did," I said. "I'd have
skinned her alive for opening a letter of mine."

Kenny smiled through a puff of cigarette smoke. "I
guess after the first one, it was easier for her to open and
read the others. Anyway, when you never answered me, I
thought that was my answer. They were pretty blunt, Mar,
my letters. Even if she was a kid, she must have known what
I was talking about."

"About us, you mean?"

He nodded. "I wanted to come back. I wanted to be
home, of course, but even if my mother wouldn't let me return here, I wanted to be with you. I guess I made it sound
pretty cornball, how I felt about you. Kids do. But the gist of
it was that, if you hated me for what I'd done, I'd understand
and I wouldn't bother you again. I left it up to you whether
you wanted to write me, whether you wanted me, too, and if
you didn't, well, then, I'd accept that."

I was angry all over again with Ingrid, realizing how
much she had interfered in something so important to me.
"She never told me," I said. "If I had known—how you
felt…"

"When I didn't hear from you, I, well, I assumed you
wanted nothing more to do with me. I didn't blame you
much. I'd acted like a bastard, anyway, that business with
Dexter, for one thing. That was childish, something I did out
of spite. And then throwing a tantrum, and running away
from home. I thought I'd burned my bridges behind me."

"But you came back anyway," I said when he paused.

"Yes," he said with a sigh. "I fought the desire, my
feelings, for five years, and in all that time, it just got worse
and worse. I wasn't happy anywhere else. Remember what a
devil-may-care little nut I was. Well, you wouldn't have
known me during those five years. Gloomy Ken, that's what
somebody nicknamed me in California, and I was, too. I
must have been the most unhappy man on earth. I was just

drifting around, without any purpose, not caring about anything.

"And then, without even realizing it at first, I started drifting this way. I didn't really plan to come back. I just found myself closer and closer, until I was in Indianapolis, and I finally realized that I was only a hundred miles or so from home. It scared me, Mar, I was almost torn in two, wanting to come back, and afraid that I'd be turned out. Afraid that you didn't want me. I still had my pride, I'm sorry to say, and I had lost a lot of my nerve."

"But how did you and Ingrid—when did you get together?"

"Luck, sheer luck," he said. They were the same words Ingrid had used to describe their meeting, but there was a world of difference in their meaning this time. "It wasn't Ingrid who saw me. It was Dexter."

"Dexter?"

"He was in Indianapolis, on business of some sort. I was working in a restaurant, as a busboy. Can you imagine that, me a busboy? I guess I didn't have too much pride. Anyway, he saw me, and I saw him. I knew who he was the minute came into the place. If I could have avoided him, I'd have done so. I wanted nothing to do with him, but I couldn't help his seeing me, so I did the next best thing: I pretended I wasn't Kenny."

"Didn't he know better?"

"At first he did. He called me by name and I ignored him as though I hadn't heard him. Then he came up and took hold of my arm, and spoke to me again. I told him he'd made a mistake and to keep his hands off me. That's when I became Douglas Allen.

"At first, he thought I was kidding him, but I have changed some. He went back to his table, but he kept staring at me and staring at me. I had been around some guys out in California, and I, well I acted kind of fruity, to throw him off. After a while, I guess he decided I really wasn't Kenny. He left and I thought I'd gotten through it all right. For a few days, nothing happened. Then, out of the blue, he came in again, but this time he had Ingrid with him. I don't know how he found her."

160

"I think I do," I told him. "They were pretty friendly, apparently. I didn't know about his being in Indianapolis, but I'd be willing to bet he was there to see her. As a matter of fact, that may have been why Ingrid wanted to go there to school in the first place."

"You mean they were lovers?"

I nodded. "She's been at his house. She left your mother's scarf there. I think that may have been part of why she was so upset when you started seeing him again. My guess is that the two of them cooked up this whole scheme together, and when you and Dexter starting getting friendly again, Ingrid must have been afraid the two of you were planning to cut her out. That's the hard part about working behind people's backs—you soon get to where you can't trust anyone else because you can't trust yourself."

I hadn't meant it to sound like criticism of him, but I realized from the way he winced that I had hit a sore spot.

"I didn't mean any harm," he said. "I've had time to regret getting involved in his business at all. But when they came in together, I recognized Ingrid, of course, but by this time I'd already told Dexter I was someone else, so I had to pretend I didn't know Ingrid either. This time, they didn't say anything to me, but I caught them staring at me all through their meal.

"That evening, when I got off work, she was waiting outside for me. She introduced herself and asked if she could talk to me for a while. It was kind of funny, actually, like a big joke, her not knowing who I really was. And besides, I was eating my heart out for some word of home. It was hard even to keep from hugging Ingrid and telling her who I was, and I wanted so much to hear about my mother, and Olsen— and you."

As he talked, it was not difficult to imagine him going through it—the scene with Ingrid, listening to her scheme, his desire, for five long years, to come home. And, of course, he'd see it as a big joke, too, on Ingrid, especially.

"I didn't like her for her schemes, but I didn't take them too seriously, either, not right away. I thought when I got here, I could always leave again or, if things went well, I could tell everybody the whole story. Ingrid would have had her lesson, and we'd all have a big laugh over it.

"But it didn't work out like that. What I hadn't realized was how much Ingrid was counting on her plans, how important they were to her. When I had been here a few days, I began to realize that his was no joke to her. She intended to get what she'd started after, by any means.

"That's when I began to hate her, and myself, for what we were doing. And I tried to call a halt to it. I told her I was going to expose the whole business. I even tried to tell her who I was, but she didn't let me get that far. She warned me that she would make a big scene, that she'd expose me for a fake—and she reminded me of my mother's health. That was what scared me. I knew she was right, that my mother might not be able to handle the shock. I thought about it, but I was afraid I might never get the chance to tell her I really was Kenny after all. So I had to keep on playing along with Ingrid, until I could come up with some way out of the jam I'd gotten myself into."

I knew I'd hate myself for asking, but one question was uppermost in my mind, and it had to be put into words. "What about Dexter?" I asked.

"I didn't know that he was in on her little scheme, I thought that was all Ingrid's idea. I figured he had simply realized, when he heard that I was back, that I was the guy he'd seen in Indianapolis, the one he'd brought Ingrid to see. He wrote me, three different letters. What they said was basically that he didn't believe I was the really Kenny, and he was going to expose me as a fraud—unless I proved to him that I was genuine."

I didn't have to ask how he was supposed to prove that. It was the same way Kenny had proven to me who he was. "Then that's why you went to him," I said, "To keep him from exposing you, and not for...."

He shook his head, but he didn't avoid my eyes. "No, that wasn't all of it. I'd have called his bluff, except that I wanted—oh, hell, Mar, I always was horny. You know that. I didn't live as any angel these last five years. And it didn't look like I was going to get—well, anyway, that was part of it. I went because I remembered that. Only, when I got there,

I couldn't. There was Dexter, and he was plenty hungry for it, only he wasn't what I wanted. I put him off."

It would have been pointless to try to hide my relief. Kenny saw it, and grinned. From the whole story, he'd finally told me what I wanted to know—or part of it, anyway.

"You tried to talk to me once," I said falteringly. "About what you'd come back for. I thought then it was the farm. But it wasn't."

"No, Mar, it wasn't. That wasn't why I came back."

We were looking straight into one another's eyes now, and I felt as if I were being drawn into those dark depths, where all the things we hadn't said were as clear and audible as what we'd put into words.

"Don't leave the farm, Ken," I said. "This is your home."

"It belongs to you now, or soon will," he said.

"On paper, maybe. But you have a much better claim to it than that.

He'd finished his cigarette. He walked to the door and threw the butt outside, letting gust of cold wind fling itself into the room. Kenny stood there in the open doorway, staring out across the snow-covered yard.

"I left, Mar," he said. "I went away from it. That makes a difference."

"Would it help if I told you that you'd never really left, not altogether? That you were always here, in my heart?"

I went across the room to stand behind him, and rest one arm lightly around his shoulders. The wind ran chill fingers through my hair. I had one argument left, and it was one I was sure he could not refuse.

"Stay here, Kenny," I said, "For me."

* * * * * * *

Ingrid left the next day. I had a good idea where she would be going, and I soon learned that I was right in my hunch. Dexter wasn't all bad, I guess. At least he married her, although as it turned out that wasn't much of a blessing for her. From all that I saw or heard, her life wasn't much happier than his last wife's had been. Olsen went to see her often, although she always came back from those visits sad and upset. I myself, except for catching glimpses of her at a distance, only saw Ingrid once up close. That was when, several years later, Olsen quietly passed on.

Ingrid came to the funeral. She looked old beyond her years, and tired, and there was little left of the prettiness she had once been so proud of. I talked to her then. I tried to make her see that she'd been forgiven for what she'd done, and that she could come home. Olsen would have wanted her to, I know, and Kenny had agreed to my making the offer.

I don't think Ingrid even heard most of what I said, though. When she had gone, she'd gone completely, and the distance from our house to Holloman's proved far greater than the distance Kenny had traveled during his absence. She never returned.

It was a fact that caused me sadness, but that, and the loss of Olsen, was very nearly the only sadness in my life. For the rest, I had one thing for which I was grateful every day of my existence, and that filled me with a never-ending sense of joy.

Kenny was back.

www.ingramcontent.com/pod-product-compliance
Lightning Source LLC
Chambersburg PA
CBHW051920240626
47153CB00004B/1296